PENGUIN CLASSICS

NETOCHKA NEZVANOVA

FYODOR MIKHAILOVICH DOSTOYEVSKY was born in Moscow in 1821, the second of a physician's seven children. When he left his private boarding school in Moscow he studied from 1838 to 1843 at the Military Engineering College in St Petersburg, graduating with officer's rank. His first story to be published, 'Poor Folk' (1846), had a great success. In 1849 he was arrested and sentenced to death for participating in the 'Petrashevsky circle': he was reprieved at the last moment but sentenced to penal servitude, and until 1854 he lived in a convict prison at Omsk, Siberia. Out of this experience he wrote *Memoirs from the House of the Dead* (1860). In 1861 he began the review *Vremya* with his brother: in 1862 and 1863 he went abroad where he strengthened his anti-European outlook, met Mlle Suslova who was the model for many of his heroines, and gave way to his passion for gambling. In the following years he fell deeply into debt, but from 1867, when he married Anna Grigoryevna Smitkina, his second wife helped to rescue him from his financial morass. They lived abroad for four years, then in 1873 he was invited to edit *Grazhdanin*, to which he contributed his *Author's Diary*. From 1876 the latter was issued separately and had a great circulation. In 1880 he delivered his famous address at the unveiling of Pushkin's memorial in Moscow: he died six months later in 1881. Most of his important works were written after 1864: *Notes from Underground* (1864), *Crime and Punishment* (1865–66), *The Gambler* (1866), *The Idiot* (1869), *The Devils* (1871), and *The Brothers Karamazov* (1880).

•

JANE KENTISH was born in 1953 and took a B.A. in Russian Literature at the University of Sussex in 1974 where two years later she gained her M.A. in Byzantine and Russian Art and Architecture. Since then she has worked as a research assistant in a London icon gallery and as a freeland translator and researcher. She does occasional lecturing in Byzantine History and Art, and has published various articles on Far and Middle Eastern Art.

FYODOR DOSTOYEVSKY

NETOCHKA
NEZVANOVA

TRANSLATED WITH AN INTRODUCTION BY
JANE KENTISH

Harry –

Happy 31st! Enjoy!

1994

PENGUIN BOOKS

PENGUIN BOOKS

Published by the Penguin Group
Penguin Books Ltd, 27 Wrights Lane, London w8 5tz, England
Viking Penguin, a division of Penguin Books USA Inc,
375 Hudson Street, New York, New York 10014, USA
Penguin Books Australia Ltd, Ringwood, Victoria, Australia
Penguin Books Canada Ltd, 2801 John Street, Markham, Ontario, Canada l3r 1b4
Penguin Books (NZ) Ltd, 182–190 Wairau Road, Auckland 10, New Zealand

Penguin Books Ltd, Registered Offices: Harmondsworth, Middlesex, England

This translation first published 1985
5 7 9 10 8 6 4

Copyright © Jane Kentish, 1985
All rights reserved

Printed in England by Clays Ltd, St Ives plc
Typeset in 9/11 pt Monophoto Photina

TRANSLATOR'S INTRODUCTION

Netochka Nezvanova, which can be loosely translated as 'nameless nobody', was Dostoyevsky's first attempt at writing a novel. The idea is first aired in the year 1846 in a letter written to his brother where he says that he intends to write a 'big novel' in the form of a 'confession'. It seems that he hoped to finish the work by the end of the following year, but the design of the novel was so ambitious and conceived on such a grandiose scale that the young writer was unable to meet all its demands; it was not until the end of 1849 that the first completed section of the book was published. This fragment, the story of a young girl's childhood, was intended as no more than a prologue to the novel. Dostoyevsky's work on it was terminated shortly after the first serialized publication; he was arrested for alleged 'revolutionary' activities as a member of the Petrashevsky group (Utopian Socialists) and subsequently imprisoned and exiled to Siberia, after being spared the firing squad at the last moment.

Neither during his period of exile nor on his return from Siberia in 1859 did Dostoyevsky resume work on *Netochka Nezvanova*. All we have is the first, unfinished section which is, however, intriguing as a record of the great author's earliest attempt to embody his thoughts and ideas in the novel form. Although *Netochka Nezvanova* lacks some of the artistic coherence of his later, more mature works, it nevertheless presents an exhaustive display of those themes which characterize Dostoyevsky's major works: grotesque pictures of both the seedy and the more noble side of Petersburg life and society; chronically sick and suffering people whose delirium and fantasy lead to a state of heightened consciousness bordering on madness; incestuous relationships; the impoverished artist struggling in a garret; murder and martyrdom; guilt and atonement for sin; the 'meek' woman and the 'proud' woman; will-power and mental inertia. All these ideas, present here in embryonic form, were explored, developed and reworked by Dostoyevsky for the rest of his literary career.

The translation of *Netochka Nezvanova* has presented certain difficulties, mainly owing to a lack of stylistic unity in the original text. The story is in autobiographical form, related by Netochka, as she recalls her childhood. Dostoyevsky makes a deliberate attempt to record and interpret events initially in the manner of a child and later in the manner of a young adult, which leads to a sharp change in the style and tone of the narration, so that it falls into three distinct and rather detached sections. This has been a source of some difficulty, since it is impossible to adopt one consistent style of translation.A further problem has been the search for an idiom appropriate to the period, for my aim has been to follow the original text as closely as possible in all respects.

Despite these difficulties it has been a most rewarding task to translate this book, particularly since it uncovers the author's earliest struggles with the form of the novel, the emergence of a style that is so typically his own and, above all, his youthful experiments with philosophical and psychological ideas and themes that become even more compelling in his later works.

1984   J.K.

CHAPTER ONE

I cannot remember my father. He died when I was two years old. My mother remarried, but it was a marriage that brought her great suffering, although she had married for love. My stepfather was a musician and was destined to lead a most remarkable life. He was the strangest and most extraordinary person I have ever known. He had too powerful an influence over my early childhood, and this certainly affected my whole life. In order to make my story more comprehensible I must first give an account of his life, the details of which I only learnt later from the famous musician B. who was a companion and close friend of my stepfather's in his youth.

My stepfather's name was Efimov. He was born in a village on the estate of a very rich landowner. He was the son of a poor musician who after many years of wandering had settled on this landowner's estate and was hired to play in his orchestra. The landowner surrounded his life with luxury and above all was passionately devoted to music. It was said of him that he had never once left his estate, not even to go to Moscow, but one day he suddenly decided to take the waters at some spa abroad and ended up by staying there for several weeks with the express purpose of listening to a famous violinist who, as he gathered from the newspapers, was giving three concerts there at the spa. He himself owned a fairly respectable orchestra on which he spent almost his entire income. It was with this orchestra that my stepfather played the clarinet.

When he was twenty-two years old my stepfather made the acquaintance of a very strange man. Living in the same district was a rich Count who had ruined himself through the upkeep of a private orchestra. The Count had dismissed the conductor of the orchestra, an Italian by birth, for misconduct. Indeed the conductor was a very bad man. After his dismissal he sank into complete degradation, frequenting the village taverns, constantly getting drunk, sometimes even begging for money, and there was certainly no one in the district anxious to employ him. It was to this man that my stepfather became a friend. It was a rather strange and vague relationship, by all accounts, since no one seemed to notice how my stepfather changed his ways somewhat under the influence of this friend. Even the landowner, who at first had forbidden him to associate with the Italian, soon turned a blind eye to them. Then, all of a sudden, the conductor died. He was found one morning by some peasants in a ditch close to a weir. An inquest was held which showed that he had died of an apoplectic fit. My stepfather, who was looking after his belongings, immediately produced evidence to show that he was fully entitled to inherit them all. The dead man had left a note written in his own hand, in which he left everything to Efimov in the event of his death. The inheritance consisted of a black tail-coat which the deceased had painstakingly preserved, since he always maintained the hope of finding work, and a rather ordinary-looking violin. No one contested the inheritance and it was not until some time later that the first violinist of the Count's orchestra appeared, bringing a letter from his master to the landowner. In the letter the Count begged him to persuade Efimov to sell him the violin left by the Italian because the Count very much wished to acquire it for his own orchestra. He offered the sum of three thousand roubles, adding that he had already on several occasions sent for Efimov in order to conduct the sale personally but Efimov had stubbornly refused to come. The Count concluded by saying that the sum he offered was an honest one, that he was not trying to get it for less than its worth and that he could only see in Efimov's obstinacy an insulting suspicion that he, the Count, was trying to take advantage of his simplicity and ignorance. He thus begged the landowner to try to bring him to reason.

The landowner instantly sent for my stepfather.

'Why don't you want to part with your violin?' he asked him. 'It's no use to you. You've been offered three thousand roubles, which is a good price. It's ridiculous to think you can get more. The Count isn't trying to trick you.'

Efimov replied that he would never go to the Count of his own accord, but that if he were sent there he would obey his master's orders. He said that he himself would never sell the violin, but that if it were taken from him by force then that again was his master's affair.

This answer made it quite clear that he had touched on one of the landowner's more sensitive spots. The landowner had always prided himself on knowing how to treat his musicians properly, for after all they were all true artists and it was to their credit that his orchestra was not only superior to the Count's but was as good as any that could be found in Moscow or Petersburg.

'Very well!' answered the landowner. 'Then I shall inform the Count that you don't wish to sell the violin because you don't feel like it and that you have the sole right to sell it or not to sell it. Is that all right? But I myself should like to ask: what use is the violin to you? Your instrument is the clarinet, although you are a poor clarinettist. Let me have it and I'll give you three thousand – whoever would have guessed it was such a valuable instrument!'

Efimov chuckled.

'No sir, I won't give it to you, unless of course you insist . . .'

'Come now, you know I won't compel you to, you know I won't use force,' shouted the landowner, who was quite beside himself, the more so since the conversation was taking place in the presence of one of the Count's musicians and he might draw some very unfavourable conclusions regarding the position of the musicians in the landowner's orchestra from witnessing this exchange.

'Be off with you, you ungrateful creature! And I don't want to set eyes on you again. And where do you think you would have got to without me, with that clarinet of yours that you cannot even play properly? I've fed you, clothed you, paid you a wage. Here you live like a gentleman – like an artist – only you choose to ignore it. Be off with you, and don't exasperate me with your presence any longer!'

The landowner always chased away anyone with whom he was angry because he was so afraid of his own temper, and not for anything in the world did he wish to be too stern with his 'artists', as he called his musicians.

So the sale did not take place, and it seemed that the matter was over when suddenly, a month later, the Count's first violinist instigated a terrible affair. Quite of his own accord he lodged a complaint against my stepfather in which he accused him of being responsible for the death of the Italian. He claimed that he had killed him because of a greedy desire to acquire his legacy. He maintained that the will had been made under duress and he promised to produce witnesses to testify to this. Neither the pleas and entreaties of the Count and the landowner, both of whom stood up for my stepfather, nor anything else that was done could deter the accuser. It was pointed out that all the medical examinations performed on the body of the dead man had been carried out quite properly and it was suggested that the accuser, in questioning the evidence, was perhaps motivated by personal malice and disappointment at not having acquired the precious instrument himself. But the man stood his ground, swearing that he was in the right and insisting that the fit had not been caused by drunkenness but through poisoning, and he demanded a second inquest. At first glance the allegations looked serious and of course the matter was put in motion. Efimov was arrested and taken off to the town prison. A trial, which aroused the interest of the whole town, began. It was over very quickly and ended in the musician being accused of giving false testimony. He was sentenced to an appropriate term but nevertheless stood his ground throughout, insisting that he was right. It was only at the very end that he admitted to not really having had any evidence, of having invented it all himself, concocting it out of supposition and guesswork. He declared that until the second inquest, when Efimov's innocence was formally proven, he had been firmly convinced that the latter had murdered the poor Italian, although he had possibly used a method other than poisoning. However, before the informer had completed his prison sentence he was suddenly taken ill with inflammation of the brain, lost his senses and died in the prison hospital.

The landowner behaved most nobly throughout the affair,

doing everything he could for my stepfather, acting as if he were his own son. He visited him in the prison several times, comforting him, giving him money and bringing him the best cigars once he discovered his partiality for smoking. When he was acquitted the whole orchestra was given a free day; the landowner saw the Efimov affair as something concerning all of them because he valued good behaviour in all his musicians as much as, if not more than, their ability.

A year had passed by when it was suddenly rumoured in the province that a certain well-known violinist, a Frenchman, had arrived in town and was intending to give a few concerts before passing on. The landowner immediately began thinking of a way to entice him to his estate. His efforts seemed successful and the Frenchman promised to come. However, just as soon as all the preparations for his visit had been made and almost the entire province notified, things suddenly took a different turn.

It was reported one morning that Efimov had disappeared, and no one knew where he had gone. A search was begun, but there was not a trace to be found. The orchestra was in an awful pickle: they had no clarinettist. Then suddenly, three days after Efimov's disappearance, the landowner received a letter from the Frenchman in which the latter haughtily declined the invitation – adding, through implication of course, that in future he would be much more careful in his relations with those gentlemen who kept their own orchestras, that it offended his aesthetic sensibility to see true talent under the control of a man who was incapable of recognizing its worth and, finally, that the example of Efimov, a genuine artist and the best violinist he had ever come across in Russia, served as sufficient proof of the truth of what he said.

The landowner was completely dumbfounded by the letter. He was profoundly mortified. What! Could it be true that Efimov, the same Efimov for whom he had gone to so much trouble and to whom he had shown so much kindness, could now so mercilessly and unscrupulously slander him, and, moreover, to a European artist whose opinion he regarded so highly? Besides, the letter was baffling in another respect: it said that Efimov was not only a talented artist but that he was a violinist whose talent had been ignored and who had been forced to play another instrument. So, astonished by all this, the landowner hastily prepared to go into town to talk to the Frenchman. At this moment, however, a letter arrived from the Count inviting him to come over to his estate immediately; he said he knew everything, and that the Frenchman was with him together with Efimov, whose audacity and slander had so stunned him that he had decided to detain him. Finally, he requested the presence of the landowner, because Efimov's remarks involved the Count himself; he said that it was an important matter that should be resolved as quickly as possible.

The landowner instantly set off to see the Count and soon made the acquaintance of the Frenchman. He publicly explained everything he knew about my stepfather, adding that he had never suspected Efimov of having any real talent; on the contrary, while in his service Efimov had never proved himself to be more than a mediocre clarinettist, and this was the first he had heard of his being a neglected violinist; he added that Efimov was a free man who had always been at liberty to leave him at any time had he really felt so oppressed. The Frenchman was surprised. They summoned Efimov, who was barely recognizable. My stepfather held himself arrogantly, answered their questions insolently and insisted on the truth of all he had managed to tell the Frenchman. All this annoyed the Count beyond belief. He told my stepfather, in no uncertain terms, that he was a rascal and a liar and fit for nothing but the most ignominious punishment.

. 'Don't excite yourself, your excellency, I know you well enough by now, oh yes, I know you well enough,' answered my stepfather. 'Thanks to you I came within an inch of being sentenced to death. And I know who it was that persuaded Alexei Nikorovitch, your former musician, to trump up a charge against me!'

These horrible accusations put the Count into a wild rage. He was barely able to control himself, but it so happened that a government official, visiting the Count on business, was in the room, and he declared that he could not let this pass without taking action. He maintained that Efimov's offensive remarks amounted to malice, wilful slander and libel and he respectfully asked permission to arrest him on the spot. Expressing tremendous indignation, the Frenchman said that he could not understand such base ingratitude, whereupon my stepfather announced that even if it was on a charge of murder any trial, any punishment, would be better than the existence he had experienced until now, living on the landowner's estate as a member of the orchestra and unable to leave before because of his extreme poverty. With these words he left the room accompanied by the man who had arrested him. He was locked in a remote room with the threat of being taken to town the following day. At about midnight the prisoner's door was opened and the landowner entered. He was wearing his nightgown and slippers and holding a lamp in his hands. It seemed that his tormenting worries had prevented him from sleeping and that he had finally been compelled to get up. Efimov, who was not sleeping either, looked up in surprise at his visitor, who put down his lamp and, deeply agitated, seated himself in a chair opposite.

'Egor,' he addressed him, 'why have you done me this injustice?'

Efimov gave no reply. The landowner repeated his question in a voice expressing deep feeling and a sort of strange grief.

'God knows,' said my stepfather eventually, making a gesture of despair. 'It must have been the devil's got inside me. I don't know myself who drove me to do it . . . But I really cannot go on living with you, I can't bear it . . . The devil himself has got inside me . . .'

'Egor!' the landowner began again. 'Come back to me. I'll forget everything, I'll forgive everything. Listen, you'll be my leading musician, you'll be paid more than anyone else . . .'

'No, sir, and please don't speak of it. It's no life for me there! I'm telling you the devil has taken hold of me. I'll set fire to your house or something if I stay. There are times when I'm overcome with such terrible despair that I wish I'd never been born. Just now I can't be responsible for my actions and you'd be better to leave me alone, sir. It all began when that fiend made a friend of me . . .'

'Who?' asked the landowner.

'Why, the one who died like a dog, snuffed it, the Italian.'

'Was it he who taught you to play, Egorushka?'

'Yes! Yes, he taught me more than enough to ruin me. I wish I'd never set eyes on him.'

'Was he really a master of the violin, Egorushka?'

'No, he wasn't much good himself, but he was a good teacher. I taught myself to play; he just showed me one or two things. But it would have been better to have lost my hand than to have learnt those things. I don't know what I want now. And you, sir, may ask: "Egorushka, what do you want – I can give you anything", and I, sir, cannot offer a single word in reply because I do not know what I want. No! I repeat, sir, it would be better for you to leave me alone. I might really go and do something to you which would get me put away for years and that would be the end of it!'

'Egor!' began the landowner after a short silence, 'I can't leave you like this. If you don't want to work for me then go, you're a free man, I won't force you to do anything. But I can't leave you like this. Play something for me, Egor, play something on your violin. For God's sake play something. I'm not ordering you to, do you understand, I'm not forcing you to, I'm only begging you, with tears in my eyes. Oh, for God's sake! Egorushka, play me the piece you played for the Frenchman. Just do this for me ... We are both being obstinate. I too have an obstinate streak, Egorushka. I can sympathize with you, but you must try to understand my feelings. I don't think I can live unless you play me the piece you played for the Frenchman. But you must do it willingly.'

'Well, all right then,' said Efimov. 'I swore to myself that I would never perform in front of you, sir, never ever before you. But my heart is melting. I'll play you something, but it will be the first time and the last time. After this you'll never hear me again, not even for a thousand roubles.'

Thereupon he picked up his violin and began playing his own variations on Russian songs. B. said that these variations were his first and his best pieces for the violin and that he never played them so well or with so much inspiration. The landowner, who always gave a display of emotion on listening to any music, was on this occasion reduced to tears. When the performance was over he got up from his chair, took out three thousand roubles and handed them to my stepfather, saying, 'Now be on your way, Egor. I am releasing you – leave it to me to settle everything with the Count. But listen a moment: you won't see me again. There is a wide road lying ahead and it would be painful for us both if we should meet. So, farewell. No, wait a little. I have just one piece of advice to give you before you start your journey: don't give way to drink but study, study as much as possible and don't let yourself grow conceited! I'm talking to you like father to son. I repeat: take care of yourself, study and keep away from the bottle. Once you start to drown your sorrows in drink – and mind you, there will be plenty of sorrow – you're as good as finished. Everything will be lost to the devil and you'll more than likely die in the ditch like that Italian friend of yours. Farewell now. Stop! One minute, kiss me.'

They embraced one another and then my stepfather walked out into freedom.

No sooner had he tasted liberty than he squandered the three thousand roubles in a nearby town where he fell into the company of the most disreputable and sordid gang of hooligans. He eventually found himself penniless, alone and with no means of earning any money. He was compelled to join a miserable band attached to a provincial travelling company as the first, and possibly the only, violinist. Of course none of this conformed to his original intention of reaching Petersburg as quickly as possible and once there studying, finding a good job, and developing his artistic talents to the full. He found life with the band uncongenial. He quarrelled with the manager and left. After this he lost heart completely and resolved to take desperate measures, although it wounded his pride terribly. He wrote a letter to the landowner explaining his predicament and asking him for money. But the letter was written in a rather arrogant manner and he received no answer. Then he wrote again, this time using the most cringing language, hailing the landowner as his true benefactor and as a supreme connoisseur of the arts;

again he asked him to send money. Finally he received an answer. The landowner sent him a hundred roubles together with a brief note written by his valet in which he asked him not to trouble him with any more requests. It was my stepfather's intention that having received the money he would set off for Petersburg at once, but after settling all his debts he found that he did not have enough money for the journey. Once again he was compelled to remain in the provinces and join a provincial band, but once again he could not get along in the company and thus ended up by continually moving on from one place to the next, always cherishing the hope that sooner or later he would reach Petersburg. Six years had passed in this way when he suddenly began to grow afraid that as a result of his chaotic and impoverished existence he was losing his talent. So one morning, abandoning his manager, he left and set off for Petersburg, almost begging his way there. He settled himself in some garret or other somewhere in Petersburg and it was there that he first met B., who had himself recently arrived from Germany and was also trying to establish a career. They soon made friends, and even to this day B. remembers the friendship with deep feeling. They were both young and had similar hopes and aspirations. However, B. was still in his first youth and had as yet suffered little hardship or sorrow, and above all he was a German through and through and strove to achieve his ambition methodically and with a great deal of perseverance. He was fully aware of the limits to his ability and was almost capable of predicting the degree of success attainable. On the other hand his companion, Efimov, was already thirty and tired and weary; his patience was spent and his health and vigour exhausted by those six years when he was forced to live a vagabond's existence moving from one provincial theatre company or band to the next, simply in order to obtain his daily bread. He had been sustained by his singular determination to quit this frightful existence and save enough money to reach Petersburg. But this had really been only a vague and rather obscure idea, a sort of irresistible inner calling which over the years had lost most of its original clarity. By the time he reached Petersburg he was acting almost unconsciously, simply following an old and familiar habit of constantly dreaming and brooding over that journey, without having very much of an idea of what he might do once he reached the capital. By now his enthusiasm was rather spasmodic, jaundiced and erratic, as if he were trying to deceive only himself, trying to convince himself that his energy, his vigour, his original inspiration and fire were not really burnt out. These fits of rapture impressed B. who, though he was cold and methodical, was blinded by them and worshipped my stepfather as the great musical genius of years to come. He could see no other future for his friend, but it was not long before his eyes were opened to the truth. He saw clearly that all his impetuosity, impatience and feverish haste amounted to nothing more than an unconscious despair at the memory of his squandered talent and that it was more than likely that this talent had never been anything very special, not even in the beginning, that there had been a great deal of blindness, of vain complacency and premature self-satisfaction, and of dreaming and fantasizing about his genius. 'But,' B. used to say, 'I couldn't help marvelling at my friend's strange temperament. I saw before my own eyes a desperate, feverish contest taking place between a violently over-strained will and inner impotence. For seven miserable years he had contented himself with mere dreams of future fame, to the extent that he failed to notice how he was losing sight of what was essential to our art and was forgetting even the most elementary mechanics of the matter. And yet in the meantime the most colossal plans for the future were taking place in his disordered mind. Not only did he wish to become a first-rate genius, to be known as one of top violinists in the world – which, incidentally, he already considered himself – but on top of all of this he dreamed of becoming a composer, although he knew nothing about counterpoint. And what astonished me most,' added B., 'was that this man, with his complete impotence and totally inadequate knowledge of musical technique, had nevertheless such a deep and lucid – one might even say instinctive – understanding of art. He had such intense feeling and appreciation for it that it is hardly surprising if he confused himself in his own mind and mistook himself for a genius, a high priest of art rather than a sympathetic, natural critic. Sometimes, in his crude and rather simple language, he would utter such profound truths that I was struck dumb and could not believe that a man who had never read anything or even studied under anyone could have worked these things out for himself. I was deeply indebted to him for my own progress and for his advice. As far as I myself was concerned I felt fairly secure about my future. I also passionately loved my art, but I knew when I embarked upon my career that I was not tremendously gifted and that I could never expect to be more than a humble labourer in the field. But still I pride myself for not behaving like the ungrateful servant. I did not bury what I was given; instead I made the best of everything I had and, if my playing and the precision of my technique is praised, I owe it to ceaseless, unending work, to a clear understanding of the limits to which I could use my talents, to voluntary self-subordination and a constant struggle against complacency, over-confidence and the laziness that is the natural consequence of such things.

B., in turn, tried to advise his friend, by whom he had been so dominated in the beginning, but he succeeded only in annoying him. The friendship began to cool off. Soon B. noticed that Efimov was increasingly overcome by apathy, grief and boredom, and his bouts of enthusiasm were becoming more and more rare, which was all leading to a state of gloomy and savage depression. And then Efimov started neglecting his violin, sometimes not touching it for weeks on end. He was verging on total moral collapse and rapidly succumbing to every vice. Exactly what the landowner had forewarned happened: he took to drink. B. looked on in horror, advising him to no avail and too afraid to reproach him. Little by little Efimov turned into an utter cynic. He had no qualms about living off B. and even behaved as if he had every right to do so. In the meantime they ran out of money. B. managed to make ends meet by giving private lessons and by performing at private evening parties given by merchants, Germans and petty officials, who paid something, though not very much. Efimov chose to ignore his friend's needs; he behaved haughtily with him and for long periods he refused to speak to him. One day, in the gentlest terms, B. pointed out that it might not be such a bad thing if he were to pay a bit of attention to his violin, in order not to forget everything. Efimov really lost his temper at this and declared that he had no intention of touching his violin again, as if supposing that someone would go down on his knees begging him to. On another occasion B. needed someone to accompany him at an evening party and asked Efimov, but the invitation only threw him into a rage. He screamed that he was no street musician and would never, like B., sink so low as to play for vulgar tradesmen who were quite incapable of appreciating his talent. B. did not utter a word in reply but Efimov, after pondering his friend's words, decided that it had been meant as a hint to point out that he was living off B. and that perhaps he too ought to be earning some money. When B. returned from the evening party Efimov began criticizing him for his meanness and declared that he would not stay with him a minute longer. And he did actually disappear for two days, although he turned up on the third acting as if nothing had happened. They went on living as before.

It was only his former friendship and attachment, not to mention his compassion for the ruined man, that prevented B. from carrying out his intention of bringing this ghastly life to an end by parting from Efimov for ever. In the end they did part. B. had a stroke of good fortune: he found an influential patron and succeeded in giving a brilliant concert performance. By this time he was already a first-rate player and his rapidly growing fame earned him a place in the orchestra of the opera house, where he soon achieved the success he deserved. When he parted from Efimov he gave him some money and with tears in his eyes begged him to return to the true path. Even now B. cannot remember him without special feeling; his friendship with Efimov had made a deep impression on his youth. They had embarked on their careers together and they had formed such an ardent attachment for one another that Efimov's strange ways, his coarse and glaring defects, had only bound B. more closely to him. B. was able to appreciate this. He saw through him and knew well in advance how it would all end up. At the farewell they wept and embraced each other.

Through his sobs Efimov confessed that he was an unfortunate man, that he was finished, that he had known it for a long time but had only now come to understand it properly.

'I have no talent!' he said, turning ash-white. This moved B. dreadfully.

'Listen, Egor Petrovitch. Whatever do you think you're doing to yourself? You can only destroy yourself with this despair. Where's your courage? Where's your patience? Now, in a fit of depression, you're saying that you have no talent: you're wrong! You have talent, I can see it from the way you can understand and appreciate music. I can show you how your whole life is a proof of it. You've told me about your earlier years and it's obvious that even then you were haunted by a similar kind of despair. And then your first teacher, the man about whom you've told me so much, aroused the first love of music in you and recognized that you have ability. You felt it just as strongly and oppressively then as you do now. The only difference is that at that time you didn't understand what was happening to you. You realized that you couldn't go on living with the landowner and yet you didn't know quite what it was you did want to do. Your teacher died too soon. He left you with just a vague yearning and, what's more important, he didn't teach you how to understand yourself. You sensed that you should be following a different path, a more ambitious one, you felt that you were destined for other things but you had no idea how to achieve them and in your misery you began to hate everything around you. But you didn't waste those six years; you studied, you thought, you became aware of yourself and your strengths. Now you're able to understand art and your vocation in art. You need patience and courage, my friend ... Achievement far greater than mine awaits you. You're a hundred times greater an artist than I, if only you had my endurance! Study and stop drinking, as your good landowner said to you. And above all make a new beginning. Begin with the basics. What is it that torments you so? Poverty? Deprivation? But it's precisely poverty and deprivation that mould the true artist. They are inevitable at the beginning. Just now no one wants you, no one is bothered about knowing you, but that's the way of the world. Just wait a while and you'll see how different it is once they've discovered you. The envy, the petty meanness and, worst of all, the stupidity will be a greater burden to you than any hardship. Talent needs sympathy and understanding, but wait until you see the sort of people who will flock around you when you've achieved just the tiniest bit of fame. All that you've gained through labour, sleepless nights, hunger and hardship will be looked on with contempt and disdain. These future friends of yours will give you neither comfort nor encouragement. They won't point out your good sides. Oh no! They'll take a malicious delight in spotting every one of your mistakes. They'll only be interested in your faults and errors. They'll celebrate over them – as if anyone could be perfect. You see, you're too conceited. Sometimes you're proud when there's no need to be and you may go and offend some important little nobody, and then there'll be trouble, for you are alone and they are many. They'll torment you; they'll prod you like a pincushion. Even I have begun experiencing all this. But now you must cheer up. You aren't completely destitute and you'll get by as long as you don't turn your nose up at humble work. Go and chop wood as I did at those evening parties. You're too impatient, it's a kind of sickness of yours. Try to be simpler – you're too subtle and you think too much; you give your brain a lot of work. You're bold with words but feeble with your bow. You're too vain and you lack fortitude. Have courage and find patience to study diligently. If you don't trust your own strength, then put your trust in luck. You still have fire and feeling. Perhaps you'll reach your goal, but, if not, trust in luck. Whichever way, you can't lose, because the stake is too great. It's a wonderful thing, my friend, to trust in luck!'

Efimov listened to his comrade with deep feeling. While the latter spoke the pallor left his cheeks; they flushed red and his eyes sparkled with unaccustomed fire, courage and hope. But this noble courage soon turned into arrogance and then to his usual impertinence, so that by the time B. had reached the end of his admonitions Efimov was already distracted and impatient. He warmly shook B. by the hand and, ever rapid in his transitions from deep self-abasement and humiliation to extreme arrogance and defiance, declared confidently that his friend need not trouble himself on his behalf, that he was perfectly capable of managing his own affairs and that very soon he would be giving a concert that would bring him instant fame and money. B. shrugged his shoulders but did not contradict him. And thus they parted, although it was not for long. Efimov was quick to spend all the money that B. had given him and came back a second, a third, a fourth time until finally on the tenth occasion B. lost patience and did not answer the door. After that they no longer saw each other.

Several years went by. Once, when B. was walking down a side-street on his way home from a rehearsal, in the entrance to a squalid tavern he bumped into a drunken, shabbily dressed man who called him by his name. It was Efimov. The man was greatly changed; his face was yellow and puffy and it was clearly visible that his dissipated life was leaving a permanent mark on him. B. was overjoyed to see him and before he had time to open his mouth he found himself being dragged into the tavern by Efimov. There, in a grimy little back-room, he started scrutinizing his friend more carefully. Efimov's clothes were in tatters, his boots worn out and his frayed shirt front was covered in wine stains. His thin hair was greying.

'What have you been doing? How did you end up here?' asked B. Efimov seemed confused and even frightened at first. He answered so jerkily and incoherently that B. wondered if he were looking at a madman. Efimov confessed that he could not talk until he had drunk some vodka but that they had long since refused him credit in the tavern. He flushed as he spoke. He tried making a gesture of reassurance but the flamboyant hand movements only produced an effect of insolence, superficiality and importunity. B. found it pitiful and, full of compassion and sympathy, he realized that his fears were justified. Nevertheless he ordered the vodka. Efimov's face was transformed with gratitude and he was so beside himself that, with tears in his eyes, he almost begged to kiss the hand of his benefactor. During dinner B. learnt that, to his great surprise, the pathetic man was married. But he was still further surprised to learn that his wife was the source of all his unhappiness and grief and that his marriage had completely destroyed his talent.

'How is that?' asked B.

'My friend, it's two years now since I've touched my violin,' said Efimov. 'She's a peasant, a cook, a coarse uneducated thing. Damn her! We do nothing but quarrel.'

'Why did you marry her, then?'

'When I met her I was starving and she had about a thousand roubles, so I rushed headlong into marriage. Mind you, she was in love with me. She grabbed me by the neck. Who forced her? The money has all gone on food and drink, brother. Eaten it. And as for my talent, gone, gone!'

B. noticed that Efimov was hurriedly trying to vindicate himself.

'I've given it all up. I've lost everything,' he added. He explained that not long before he had nearly reached perfection on the violin and that although B. might be said to be one of the finest violinists in town, he could outshine him completely.

'Then what's your problem?' said B. 'You should have found a good post.'

'It's not worth it!' cried Efimov, waving his hands in the air. 'Is there no one who can understand anything! What do you know? Rubbish! Nothing! That's what you know! Strumming a dance tune for some ballet, that's your kind of work. You've never seen or heard a decent violinist. What's the point in talking to you? Carry on as you are!' With this, Efimov gesticulated again and lurched forwards drunkenly in his chair. Then he began inviting B. to stay with him, but the latter declined, took his address and promised to come and see him the following day. Efimov, who had by this time eaten his fill, was glancing mockingly at his friend, trying his best to wound him. As they were leaving he grabbed hold of B.'s expensive fur coat and handled it like a grovelling servant. As they passed through the outer room he introduced him to the innkeeper and patrons as one of the first and foremost violinists in the capital. In short, his behaviour was extremely repulsive.

B. did, however, seek him out the following morning, finding him in the one-roomed attic where we were living at this time

23

in great poverty. I was four years old then and my mother had been married to Efimov for two years. She was an unhappy woman. Formerly she had worked as a governess, and she was well educated and attractive. She had married my father, an elderly government official, because she was poor. But she only spent a year with him. My father died suddenly, leaving a meagre inheritance which was divided among his heirs. My mother was left on her own with me and only a small sum of money, her share of the inheritance. With a small child to take care of, it was difficult for her to get another position as a governess. It was at this point that she happened to meet Efimov and she really did fall in love with him. She was an enthusiast and a dreamer, who saw in Efimov some kind of genius, and she believed his arrogant talk of a brilliant future. She was flattered by the glamorous image of becoming the firm guiding hand and support of a genius, and she married him.

All her hopes and dreams vanished within a month and she was forced to face the pitiful reality. Efimov, who had more than probably married her because she had a thousand roubles, sat back and folded his arms after the money was spent, and, as if glad of an excuse, declared to all and sundry that marriage was the death of talent, that he could not work in a stuffy room face to face with a starving family, that these surroundings were not conducive to inspiration and that it was clear that he was destined for this kind of misfortune. It seems that he himself had come to believe in the truth of what he was saying and was only too pleased to find another line of defence. The unhappy, ruined genius was searching for an inner cause on which to put the blame for his misfortune and disaster.

He did not seem capable of accepting the fact that he had long ago irreversibly lost his chance of becoming an artist. He struggled convulsively with this terrible conviction, as with a deadly nightmare, and when at last reality overwhelmed him, when his eyes were opened for just a minute, he almost went crazy with fear. It was not easy for him to forget everything that had for so long given a meaning to his life and until the final moment he believed that all hope was not yet lost. In times of doubt he gave himself up to drunkenness, which drove away

24

his grief, drowning his sorrows with intoxicating fumes. I do not think he ever realized how necessary his wife was to him at that time. She was a living pretext and, in truth, my stepfather never moved from his conviction that once he had buried his wife, *who had ruined him*, everything would be put right. My poor mother did not understand him. Like the true dreamer, she broke down at the first contact with reality. She became hot-tempered, irritable and shrewish, and was always quarrelling with her husband, who in his turn delighted in tormenting her; and she was continually badgering him to work. But my stepfather's blind obsession, his irrationality and his mental wanderings made him almost inhuman and unfeeling. He used to laugh and swear that he would not touch his violin again until his wife was dead, and he even told her this with a cruel frankness. My mother, who loved him despite everything right up to her death, simply could not endure this life. She became chronically ill, lived in perpetual torment and suffering, and on top of all this misery the anxiety of maintaining a family rested on her shoulders alone. She began preparing food at home and started a kind of service whereby people could come and collect their food, but Efimov stole her money on the sly and she often found herself compelled to send her customers' dishes back empty. When B. visited us she was busy washing linen and remaking old clothes. In this way we managed to live, from hand to mouth, in our attic.

B. was struck by our poverty.

'Listen, you're talking utter nonsense,' he said to my stepfather. 'Where is this destroyed talent? She's keeping you, what are you doing?'

'Nothing!' answered my stepfather.

B. had yet to learn of all my mother's troubles. Her husband often brought home whole gangs of drunkards and ragamuffins and then all hell was let loose!

B. spent a long time trying to persuade his old friend; finally he told him that if he would do nothing to mend his ways there was no point in trying to help him. He told him quite bluntly that he was not going to give him any money because it would only be spent on drink. He asked him to play something on the violin so that he might see what could be done for him on that level. While my stepfather was fetching his violin, B. secretly handed some money to my mother, but she would not take it. She had never before been asked to accept charity! B. then gave it to me and my poor mother burst into tears. My stepfather returned with the violin but instantly demanded some vodka, saying that he could not play without it. The vodka was sent for. He drank it and mellowed.

'I'll play you something of my own, since you're a friend,' he said to B., pulling a thick, dusty exercise book out from the chest of drawers.

'I wrote all that myself,' he said, pointing at the book. 'There, you see, my friend, it's very different from your ballets.'

B. studied a few pages in silence and then unfolded the music he had brought with him and asked my stepfather to forget his own compositions and to play something he had brought instead.

My stepfather was a little offended but, fearing to lose his new benefactor, he complied. B. realized that his friend really had been studying and had made considerable progress since the last parting, despite his boast of not having touched his violin since he married. It was such joy to see my poor mother's face. She looked at my stepfather and felt proud of him again. B. too was genuinely pleased and resolved to try to fix him up with a job. He already had a great many connections and he promptly began getting in touch with them, recommending his poor friend from whom he had obtained a promise to behave. Meanwhile, at his own expense, he equipped Efimov with proper clothes and took him to see several prominent people upon whom the appointment could depend. The truth was that Efimov's bravado was nothing but empty talk and he was only too pleased to follow his friend's proposals. B. told me that the flattery and cringing obsequiousness with which my stepfather tried to conciliate him for fear of losing his good fortune was embarrassing. Aware that he was being set on the right path, Efimov even gave up drinking and finally managed to get a position in the theatre orchestra. He made good use of the opportunity and after one month of hard work and diligence he regained all that he had lost in a year and a half's worth of laziness. He promised that from then onwards he would be honest and meticulous in the performance of his duties. But our family situation did not improve at all. My stepfather did not give my mother a copeck out of his salary; he spent it all on himself, eating and drinking with his new companions, of which he soon had a regular circle. He mostly mixed with theatre people: attendants, chorus singers and extras – in other words with those among whom he felt superior and not with people of any talent. He succeeded in inspiring them with a special kind of respect for himself; he immediately impressed upon them that he was a neglected man, that he had enormous talent but that his wife had destroyed it, and, finally, that their conductor knew absolutely nothing about music. He laughed at all the other members of the orchestra, at the selection of plays produced and even at the composers of the operas performed. Finally he began to propound a new theory of music and succeeded in boring everyone around him. He quarrelled with his colleagues and with the conductor; he was rude to the manager and generally acquired a reputation for being the most troublesome, the most cantankerous and the most worthless of men. Everyone found him insufferable.

Indeed it was very strange to see such an insignificant man, such a stupid and useless performer, such a negligent musician full of such vast pretences, boasts, conceits and ugly manners.

It all came to an end when he quarrelled with B. Efimov had concocted and circularized some very ugly gossip and horrible slander concerning him. After six months of unsatisfactory service he was dismissed from the orchestra on charges of drunkenness and laziness. But it proved more difficult to get rid of him. He soon reappeared, dressed in his former rags, for his decent clothes were all sold or pawned. He started loafing about with his former workmates, indifferent to whether they were pleased to see him or not. He spread spiteful gossip, babbled nonsense, wept over his miserable predicament and invited them all to come and see for themselves what a diabolical wife he had.

Of course he found an audience, those who took pleasure in offering a drink to a dismissed colleague, and they made him talk all kinds of rubbish. Moreover he always spoke poignantly and wittily, filling his talk with caustic quips and cynical digressions, which pleases a certain type of listener. He was taken for a crackpot fool who could at times be made to chatter if there was nothing better to do. They enjoyed provoking him by talking about some new violinist about to arrive in Petersburg. Whenever he heard this, Efimov's face would fall; he would grow diffident and try to discover who it was that was coming and whether or not he was talented. He always became very envious. I believe it was at this time that his real, permanent madness set in; he had an unshakeable belief that he was the finest violinist in Petersburg but was persecuted by ill luck and that owing to various intrigues he had been misunderstood and left in obscurity. He flattered himself with this notion because he was one of those people who are very fond of seeing themselves among the insulted and injured, of complaining aloud about it and finding secret comfort in gloating over their unrecognized genius. He knew the names of all the violinists in Petersburg and he did not consider one of them to be a rival. Connoisseurs and dilettantes who knew the unfortunate madman enjoyed talking in front of him about some respected violinist, simply to see his reactions. They enjoyed his malicious, impertinent remarks and they liked the apt and rather clever things he said in criticism of his imaginary rivals. They were frequently unable to understand him, but they were convinced that no one else could so audaciously and smartly caricature the musical celebrities of the day. Even the musicians he mocked were a little afraid of him, for they knew his biting wit. They recognized the pertinence of his attacks and the aptness of his judgements in the instances where criticism was valid. And they grew accustomed to seeing him in the corridors of the theatre and behind the scenes. The attendants allowed him to wander around as freely as if he were indispensable and he became something of a household Thersites. This continued for two or three years until finally everyone grew bored with him again. He was completely ostracized, and during the last two years of his life he disappeared like a fish in the ocean, never to be seen again. B., however, stumbled across him a couple of times but in such a pitiful plight that again his compassion prevailed over repugnance. He called out his name, but my stepfather felt so mortified that he pretended not to hear, pulled his battered hat down over his eyes and passed by. At last, on the morning of an important holiday B. was informed that his former friend, Efimov, had come with his greetings. B. went out to see him. Efimov stood there drunk and began making extremely low bows, almost to the ground, and – murmuring something inaudibly – refused to enter the house. It was as if he were saying: 'How can the likes of me mix with important people like you? The lackey's place will do for us. We can greet you and be off.' The whole affair was very obscene, silly and revoltingly offensive. After that B. did not see him again, not until the time of the catastrophe that ended this miserable, morbid, delirious life.

It all ended in a very strange way. The catastrophe is closely related not only to my first childhood impressions, but also to all the rest of my life. This is what happened . . . But first I must explain the sort of childhood I had and what sort of person it was who left such a torturous mark on my early memories and was also the cause of my poor mother's death.

CHAPTER TWO

I cannot remember my life before the age of about nine. I do not know quite why, but nothing that happened before then left a very strong impression. From the time when I was eight and a half I begin to remember everything very clearly, day by day without a break, as if it all happened only yesterday. It is true there are one or two things I can remember from my early childhood, but in a dreamlike fashion – a little lamp always burning before an old-fashioned icon in a dark corner of the room; then being knocked down in the street by a horse, after which I am told I lay ill for three months; then, too, times during that illness when I would wake up in the night, lying beside my mother in her bed and frightened by morbid dreams, by the stillness of the night and by the mice scratching in the corner, and all the time trembling with fear, huddling terrified under the bedclothes but never daring to wake her up – from which I concluded that my fear of her was the greatest terror. But from that moment when I suddenly became aware of myself I developed remarkably quickly and was more than capable of contending with many unchildlike impressions. Everything became clear to me and I understood things swiftly and easily. The feelings I remember well are vivid and miserable; it was these feelings I began experiencing every day, growing stronger and stronger as time went by and leaving indelible impressions. The whole time during which I lived with my parents is shrouded in a strange gloomy colour, as is my entire childhood.

It feels now as if I had suddenly become conscious, as if I had woken from a deep sleep (although at the time, of course, the change cannot have been so startling). I found myself in a large low-ceilinged room that was dusty and dirty. The walls were coloured a dirty grey; in the corner stood a large Russian stove; the windows looked out on the street, or more accurately on the roof of the house opposite, and were short and broad like chinks. The windowsills were so high above the floor that I remember having to push a table and chair underneath them in order to clamber up to the window. I was very fond of sitting there when no one was at home. Since the room was the attic of a big six-storeyed house I could see half the town from it. Our furniture consisted of nothing but the remains of an oilcloth sofa with the stuffing coming out and covered in dust, a simple white table, two chairs, my mother's bed, a little corner cupboard with something in it, a chest of drawers which always stood tilted to one side and a torn paper screen.

I remember it was dusk; everything was in a disordered mess – brushes, rags, wooden bowls, a broken bottle and God knows what else. I remember that my mother was terribly excited and crying about something. My stepfather was sitting in the corner dressed in the tattered frock-coat he always wore. He made some sarcastic remark which made her angrier than ever, and then the brushes and bowls began to fly. I burst into tears, screaming and rushing over to them both. I was in a terrible state of panic and clung tightly to my stepfather to protect him. Goodness knows why, but I felt that my mother had no reason to be angry with him, that he was not to blame, and I wanted to beg forgiveness for him and bear whatever punishment myself. I was dreadfully afraid of my mother and presumed that everyone was. At first she was stunned by my behaviour and then, grabbing me by the arm, she dragged me behind the screen. I knocked my arm rather painfully against the bedstead, but my terror was greater than the pain and I did not even wince. I remember too that my mother began speaking to my father, heatedly and bitterly, and pointing at me (from now onwards I shall refer to my stepfather as my father, for it was actually much later on that I discovered he was not my real father). This whole scene lasted a couple of hours; shaking in anticipation, I tried as hard as I could to guess how it would all end up. At last the arguing subsided and mother went out somewhere. Then my father called me to him, kissed me, stroked my hair, put me on his knee and let me nestle close to him. It was, I suppose, the first time I had received any parental caress and perhaps that is why I started, from that moment, to re-member everything so distinctly. I realized too that I had won my father's favour through defending him and for the first time it occurred to me that he had a great deal to put up with from my mother. That idea stayed with me, troubling me more and more by the day.

From that moment there arose in me a boundless love for my father, but it was a strange sort of love, not a childlike feeling. I would say that it was more like a compassionate *motherly* feel-ing, if one can use that expression of a child! My father always seemed to me so pitiful, so unbearably tormented, such a crushed creature and so full of suffering that it would have been horribly unnatural for me not to have loved him passion-ately, not to have comforted him and been tender towards him, not to have done everything possible for him. But even now I cannot understand how I got the idea into my head that my father was such a martyr and the unhappiest man in the world. Whatever can have inspired that idea! How could I, a child, have had any understanding of his personal misfortunes? Yet in my own way I did understand something, although it all became twisted and refashioned in my imagination. But still today I cannot conceive how I came to have these impressions. Perhaps my mother was a bit too stern with me and so I clung to my father as if to a fellow-sufferer.

I have already described my first awakening from childhood sleep; my first engagement with life. My heart was wounded from the very beginning and my development began with in-comprehensible and exhausting rapidity. I was no longer satis-fied by external impressions alone and I began to think, to reason, to observe. But these faculties were put into use at such an unnaturally early age that my mind could not really inter-pret things properly and I found myself living in a world of my own. Everything around me started turning into the fairy tale which my father frequently told me and which I interpreted as reality. A strange idea arose in me. I became fully aware, al-though I do not know how it came about, that I was living in an unusual family situation and that my parents were quite unlike any of the other people whom I chanced to meet. 'Why,'

I used to wonder, 'why are other people so unlike my parents, even in appearance? Why do I see laughter on the faces of others, while in our little corner no one laughs or shows any happiness? What power, what force has caused me, a child of nine, to analyse every word spoken to me by anyone I chance to meet on the stairs, or in the street when, wrapping mother's old jacket around me to cover my rags, I go out with a few copecks to buy the odd ounce of sugar, tea or bread?' I understood, and again I do not know how I came to understand, that there was an everlasting, unbearable air of sorrow in our attic room. I searched for an answer and I do not know who it was that helped me to unravel the riddle in the way I did. I blamed my mother and I saw her as my father's evil genius, but, I repeat, I have no idea how such a monstrous image developed. And the more attached I grew to my father the more I came to loathe my mother. Still now this memory torments me sorely. There was another incident which, even more than the first, contributed to this strange devotion I had for my father. One day, at about nine o'clock in the evening, my mother sent me to the shop to buy some yeast. My father was not at home. On the way back I slipped in the street and spilled the whole cupful. The first thing that came to my mind was my mother's wrath, but at the same time I felt a horrible pain in my left arm and I could not get up. Passers-by gathered around me; an old woman was helping me and a boy running by knocked my head with a key. At last I was on my feet. I picked up the fragments of broken cup and set off, swaying and staggering, when I suddenly caught sight of my father. He was standing in a crowd before a grand house opposite our lodgings. The house belonged to a well-to-do family and was splendidly illuminated. A number of carriages had driven up to the entrance, and strains of music drifted down from the windows into the street. I clutched my father by the tails of his frock-coat, pointed to the pieces of broken cup and began tearfully telling him that I was afraid of going back to mother. I felt sure he would stand up for me. But why, I wonder, was I so sure that he loved me more than my mother did? Why was it that I could approach him without fear? Taking me by the hand, he began comforting me and

33

then, lifting me up in his arms, he said he wanted to show me something. He was holding me by my bruised arm, which hurt terribly, and I was unable to see anything. But I did not cry, through fear of offending him. He kept asking me whether I could see anything and, doing my utmost to give him an answer that would please him, I said that I could see some red curtains. He wanted to carry me over to the other side of the street, closer to the house, when suddenly, I don't know why, I started crying, hugging him and begging to be taken to mother. I remember that at the time my father's caresses were upsetting me and I could not bear the thought that one of the two people whom I so longed to love did love me and treated me kindly, while the other intimidated me and made me afraid of even approaching her. However, my mother was hardly angry at all and immediately sent me to bed. I remember that the pain in my arm grew worse and worse, making me feverish, and yet I was particularly happy because it had all turned out so well. I dreamed of the house with the red curtains throughout the night.

When I woke up the following day my first thought and concern was for the house with the red curtains. As soon as mother had gone outside I clambered up to the little window and gazed out at the house. For a long time it had fascinated my childish curiosity. I particularly liked looking at it in the evening when the street was lit up and the crimson-red curtains behind the plate-glass windows gleamed with a peculiar blood-red glow. Sumptuous carriages, drawn by handsome proud horses, were continually driving up to the front door, and everything aroused my curiosity: the clamour and commotion at the entrance, the different-coloured lamps of the carriages and the lavishly dressed women who drove up in them. In my child's imagination all this assumed an image of regal magnificence and fairy-tale enchantment. However, after the encounter with my father outside the house, it all became doubly magical and intriguing. My inflamed imagination started conjuring up the most incredible thoughts and suppositions. And it is hardly surprising that, living as I did amid two people as strange as my father and mother, I did become a rather unusual and peculiar child. I was always struck by the contrast in their characters, the way, for instance, that my mother fussed incessantly and worried over our miserable household, reproaching my father for the fact that it was she alone who provided for us all. I could not help asking why he did nothing to help her, why he lived like a stranger in the house. I gained a little insight from some of the things my mother said and it was with surprise that I learnt that my father was an artist (the word stuck in my mind) and a man of genius. I soon formed a clear concept of an artist as being a man unique and apart from the others. Possibly my father's behaviour contributed to this idea. There was something he once said that made an exceptionally strong impression upon me. He said: 'The time will come when I shall no longer live in poverty, when I shall be a gentleman. When mother dies I shall be born again.' I remember how these words frightened me terribly at first. I could not bear to stay in the same room as him and ran out into the chilly hallway, where I leant against a windowsill, buried my face in my hands and sobbed. Later on, when I thought it over and reconciled myself to my father's terrible wish, my wild imagination came to my assistance. I could not be tormented by uncertainty for long and had to reach some mode of acceptance. And so – goodness knows how it all began – I fastened on to the idea that when my mother died my father would leave this miserable attic room and go away somewhere, taking me with him. But where? Not even my fantasy could find an answer to that. I only remember that I used to dream of adorning this place with the most brilliant, luxurious and splendid things that my mind could conjure. It seemed to me that we would soon be rich. I would not be sent on errands to the shops, which I always found very burdensome because the children living next door invariably teased me when I left the house, and I would be so nervous, especially if I was carrying milk or oil, knowing that, if I spilt it, I would pay for it dearly. Then I resolved, dreaming, that my father would immediately dress himself well and we would move into a magnificent house. And here the grand house with the crimson curtains, and the experience there with my father, came to the assistance of my imagination. And I soon conjectured everything in terms of moving to that house and enjoying uninterrupted peace and comfort. From then on I used to look out of the window in the evenings, gazing with intense curiosity at the enchanted house, familiarizing myself with the flow of visitors, who were dressed with an elegance and refinement such as I had never seen before. I imagined the harmonious strains of music drifting through the windows and I watched the shadows flitting across the curtains, always trying to guess what was going on there and always convinced that this was the realm of paradise and eternal joy. I loathed our miserable lodgings and the rags I had to wear. One day my mother scolded me and ordered me to come down from the window. It was then that the idea occurred to me that she disliked my looking at that house, that she did not want me to think about it, that she disliked the thought of our happiness and wanted to interfere even with this ... I looked at mother intently and suspiciously for the rest of the evening.

How did I develop such cruel feelings towards a creature who suffered so eternally as my mother? It is only now that I begin to understand what a misery her life was, and I cannot think of her tortured existence without feeling pain in my heart. Even then, in that dark strange period of my childhood, a period of quite abnormal development, my heart often ached from pain and pity; fear, confusion and doubt weighed heavily on my soul. Pangs of conscience and self-reproach rose up within me and I felt distressed and miserable on account of my unjust feelings towards my mother. For some reason we were estranged from one another and I cannot remember feeling affectionate towards her. To this day there are some trifling memories that still lacerate my heart. I remember how once (and what I am now describing is trivial and elementary and not really of a great deal of importance, but it is nevertheless precisely these kinds of memories that particularly torment me and are most painfully imprinted on my mind), one evening when my father was not at home, my mother sent me to the shop to buy her some tea and some sugar. She kept hesitating, changing her mind and counting over her copecks as she tried to calculate the pitiful sum she could afford to spend. I think she must have spent nearly half an hour counting them and still she could not work it out satisfactorily. At times she sunk into a kind of stupor and kept on repeating something, counting aloud in a low monotonous voice as if the words were falling out of her mouth by themselves. Her lips and her cheeks were pale, her hands trembled and she kept on shaking her head, as she thought in solitude.

'No, it isn't necessary,' she said, glancing at me. 'I ought really to go to bed, don't you think? Are you sleepy, Netochka?' I did not answer; she lifted my head and looked at me so sweetly and tenderly, her own face glowing with such a warm maternal smile, that my heart throbbed violently. Besides, she had called me Netochka, from which I could tell that she was feeling particularly fond of me. She had herself coined that name as an affectionate version of Anna, and when she used it I knew she was feeling close to me. I was so moved that I felt a strong urge to hug her, to cling to her and weep with her. For a long time the poor woman continued to stroke my hair almost mechanically, hardly knowing what she was doing and repeating: 'My child, Annetta, Netochka.' The tears were streaming down my face and it required effort to control them. I stubbornly refused to let go and display my feelings. I do not believe that this kind of cruelty was natural to me, or that her severity could have turned me against her in this way. No! I was tainted by my fantastic, exclusive love for my father. Sometimes, while I was falling asleep, huddling beneath the chilly covers on my little bed in the corner, I would begin to feel somehow strange. Memories would rise up in my mind, memories of when I was smaller, not so long ago, when I used to sleep in mother's bed and was less afraid of waking up in the night, for I could wriggle up to her, squeezing my eyes tightly closed, and cling firmly to her until I fell asleep again. I still felt that I could not help secretly loving her. I have noticed that many children are abnormally unfeeling and if they do love one person it tends to be to the exclusion of others. And that is how it was with me.

Sometimes there was a death-like silence in our attic for weeks on end. My father and mother would cease quarrelling and I would live with them as before, always silent, broody, fretting, and trying to reach somewhere else in my dreams. Watching them together, I could fully understand their relationship with one another. I realized that there was a vague but permanent antagonism between them, which produced an atmosphere of grief and disorder that permeated our life. Of course I only understood it to the extent I was capable of at that time, without grasping the cause and the effect. At times, during the long winter evenings, forgotten in my corner, I would avidly watch them for hours, gazing into my father's face and trying to guess his thoughts. My mother sometimes startled and frightened me. She would pace up and down the room for hours without stopping. She even did it in the night when, tormented by insomnia, she used to get up and start pacing, mumbling away to herself as if she were alone, flinging her arms in the air, folding them across her bosom, or wringing her hands in an expression of dreadful, exhausting grief. At times the tears flowed down her face, probably tears that had no specific meaning to her. And at times she collapsed in a state of oblivion. She was suffering from a very serious disease that she neglected entirely.

I remember that my own loneliness and the silence I dared not break became increasingly oppressive. For a whole year I had been living an interior life, always thinking, dreaming and secretly tormented by the unintelligible and obscure impulses that were developing inside me. I was as wild as a forest animal. Finally my father began to take notice of me; he called me over to him and asked why I stared at him so much. I do not remember what answer I gave, but I do remember that he thought a little and eventually said that tomorrow he would teach me the alphabet, so that I could read. I awaited this event impatiently and dreamt about it all night without really knowing what an alphabet was. The next day my father did in fact begin teaching me. Quickly grasping what was required of me, I learnt rapidly, for I knew that this would please him. It was the happiest time of my life. When he praised me for my intelligence, stroked my hair and kissed me I almost wept for joy. My father gradually grew fond of me and I became less afraid of speaking to him. Sometimes we talked for hours, never growing weary,

38

although I frequently failed to understand a word of what he said to me. But I was a little afraid of him, afraid he might think I was bored with him, and so I did all that was possible to pretend I understood everything. It became a habit between us to sit down together in the evenings. As soon as it began to grow dark and he came home, I went to him at once with my reading book. He would sit me down opposite him on a little footstool and after the lesson he used to read to me. Without understanding anything I kept laughing and laughing, hoping to please him by doing so. It amused him to see me laugh and he would grow more cheerful. One day after the lesson he told me a fairy tale. It was the first tale I had ever heard. I sat spellbound. I followed the story with great excitement and found myself drifting off into another world. By the time the story reached its end I was quite ecstatic. It was not so much the story that produced this effect as the fact that I took it to be true and, giving free rein to my elaborate fantasy, I confused fact and fiction. I constantly conjured up the house with the crimson curtains and somehow my father appeared as a character in the story (goodness knows how, since he was reading it), and my mother was there too, doing something or other in order to prevent my father and me from going off together, I do not know where; and I too was taking part, with my incredible daydreams and my brain brimming with the wildest and most impossible phantoms. All this was so muddled and confused in my mind that it soon turned into utter chaos. For a time I completely lost my faculties of judgement, all sense of time and reality disappeared, and I have no idea where I thought I was. I was longing to speak to my father about what the future held for us, what he was waiting for and where he was going to take me when we finally abandoned the attic room. I felt quite sure that all this was about to happen, but how and in what way it would be achieved I had no idea, and I only made myself suffer more through worrying about it. Sometimes, usually in the evening, I felt that at any moment my father might give a furtive wink, indicating that I must go out into the passage; I imagined myself creeping past my mother, picking up my book and the one and only picture – a wretched old lithograph that

had been hanging, unframed, on the wall since time im-
memorial and which I had firmly decided to take with us – and
then we would run away together and never see mother again.
One day when mother was out I chose a moment when father
seemed to be in a good mood, which was usually after he had
been drinking, went up to him and began talking about
something, intending to steer the subject towards my cherished
plan. Once I had succeeded in making him laugh, warmly embracing him and trembling in anticipation of the alarming
things I was about to say, I began questioning him in a muddled
and confused manner: When and where would we be going?
What should we take with us? How would we live? And would
it be in the house with the red curtains?

'House? Red curtains? What do you mean? What nonsense is
this, my silly one?'

More frightened than ever, I started explaining to him that
when mother died we would no longer need to live in the attic
room and he could take me somewhere where we would be
rich and happy, and I assured him that he had promised this to
me. In trying to convince him I managed to convince myself
that this was what he had actually said, or at any rate what I
believed him to have said.

'Mother dead? When mother is dead?' he repeated, looking at
me in amazement and knitting his thick grey eyebrows as his
expression changed. 'What are you saying, you poor foolish . . .?'
Then he began to scold me and spent a long time telling me
that I was a silly child and that I understood nothing. I
cannot remember all that he said but I know he was very
distressed.

I did not understand a word of his reproaches, nor did I
appreciate how it pained him to know that I must have overheard and thought about things he had said to my mother in
moments of rage and deep despair. Whatever feelings of madness and rage might have been running through him at the
time, this must, naturally, have been a shock to him. As for me,
although I did not know what was making him so angry, I was
nevertheless very upset and hurt and I started to cry. It seemed
as if all that was awaiting us was so important that a silly child

like me dare not speak or think about it. Moreover, although I did not realize this immediately, I did, in a vague way, feel that I had wronged my mother. I was overwhelmed with fear; terror and doubt were creeping into my heart. Seeing that I was crying and suffering, he began comforting me, wiping away the tears with his sleeve and beseeching me not to cry. We sat together in silence for a long while: he frowned and seemed to be pondering something; he began to speak to me again but, however hard I tried, everything he said remained very unclear. From certain sentences and phrases I was forced to conclude that he must have been trying to explain to me that he was a great artist, that no one understood him and that he was really a remarkably talented man. I recall too that, after asking whether I understood and receiving a satisfactory answer, he made me repeat 'talented', after which he laughed a little, for perhaps in the end he himself was amused that he should have talked to me of a matter so crucial to him. Our conversation was interrupted by the arrival of Karl Fyodorovitch. I instantly forgot what had just happened and burst into gay laughter as father pointed to him saying: 'Now Karl Fyodorovitch here hasn't got a copeck's worth of talent.'

This Karl Fyodorovitch was a very interesting person. I saw so few people during this period of my life that I could not possibly have forgotten him. I can see him today: he was a German by the name of Meyer. He had been born in Germany but had left in order to come to Russia, where he desperately hoped to join a Petersburg ballet company. But he was a very poor dancer and failed to find work, even in the *corps de ballet*, and ended up as an extra in a theatre company. He played various non-speaking parts, such as in one of the 'Fortinbras' suites – he played one of the knights of Verona who lift their banners, all twenty of them in unison, crying, 'We will die for our king!' Yet there was certainly no actor in the world more passionately devoted to his parts than Karl Fyodorovitch. The worst misfortune and sorrow in his life was that he could not get into the ballet. He put the art of ballet above all others in the world, and in his own way he was as dedicated to it as my father was to his violin. He had made friends with my father

41

when they were both working at the theatre, and since then the unsuccessful dancer had never forgotten him. They often saw one another and used to commiserate about their unlucky plight and their failure to be recognized. The German was the most sensitive and gentle man in the world and the friendship he offered my father was passionate and selfless. I imagine that my father was not particularly attached to him and only put up with him for lack of better company. Besides, my father's attitude was so exclusive that he could not see that the art of ballet was an art at all, which reduced the German to tears. Knowing his weak spot, he always touched it and laughed at the unfortunate Karl Fyodorovitch when the latter grew excited and tried to defend himself. I later heard a lot more about him from B., who always called him 'the Nuremberg upstart'. B. told me that time and again, while the two of them were drinking together, they would start bewailing their misfortunes in being unrecognized. I remember such occasions; I used to start whimpering, I do not know why. It always happened when mother was not at home: the German was dreadfully afraid of her – he used always to stand and wait outside in the passage until somebody came out and, if he learnt that mother was at home, would quickly run downstairs again. He always brought some German poetry along with him and grew terribly excited upon reading it aloud to us. And then, for our benefit, he would translate it and read it again in Russian. This amused father greatly and made me laugh until I cried. Once they got hold of something in Russian which excited them to such an extent that from then onwards they almost always read it together when they met. It was a drama in verse by a famous Russian writer. The opening lines became so familiar to me that when I came across them some years later I recognized them without difficulty. The drama concerned the misfortunes of a certain great painter called Gennaro or Giaccobi, who cried out on one page, 'No one recognizes me!' or on another, 'I am famous!' or 'I have no talent!' and a few lines later 'I am talented!' It all ended most pathetically. The play was, naturally, a very poor one but it affected the two readers in the most naïve and tragic way because they found in the leading characters a strong resemblance to themselves.

There were occasions when Karl Fyodorovitch became so impassioned that he would leap up from his chair, rush over to the opposite corner of the room and, throwing himself at my father and myself, calling me *mademoiselle*, implore and beg us, with tears in his eyes, to decide his fate then and there. Thereupon he would start to dance, calling out as he performed certain steps and asking us to tell him instantly whether or not he was an artist. Father was always highly amused and used secretly to wink at me out of the corner of his eye, as if to say that he would make good fun of the German. I was tremendously amused, but father would hold up his hand warning me to regain control and stifle my laughter. Even now I smile as I remember it. I can still see that poor Karl Fyodorovitch: a very small, thin, grey-haired man with a red hooked nose stained with snuff, and hideous bow legs of which he nevertheless seemed proud, since he used to wear tightly fitting trousers over them. Whenever he came to the end of his dance he would stand poised, holding out his hands to us and smiling in the way that dancers smile on the stage at the end of a performance. For a while father would keep quiet, as if unable to make up his mind enough to pronounce judgement, thus purposely leaving the unrecognized dancer in his pose, swaying from side to side in an attempt to maintain his balance. Finally father would glance at me with a very serious expression, as if inviting me to be an impartial witness to his judgement. At the same time the timid beseeching look of the dancer was fixed on me.

'No, Karl Fyodorovitch, you have not done it!' father would say, pretending that he found it unpleasant to utter the bitter truth. Then a genuine groan would break forth from Karl Fyodorovitch, but in a second he recovered himself and with even more rapid gestures he would once again beg our attention and, assuring us that his previous method had been mistaken, would plead for another chance. Then off he went again to the other side of the room, leaping into the air with such fervour that he sometimes hit his head against the ceiling and bruised himself quite painfully. Bearing the pain like a Spartan, he continued to dance, ending up in the same pose, arms outstretched and a smile across his face. Then he begged us to decide his fate. But my father was relentless and answered as despondently as before: 'No, Karl Fyodorovitch. It must be fate: you have not done it!'

At this point I could no longer restrain myself and broke into peals of laughter. My father joined in. Finally, noticing that we were laughing at him, Karl Fyodorovitch flushed scarlet with indignation and his eyes filled with tears. In a voice expressing ridiculous emotion, making me feel guilty afterwards, he said to father, 'You're a rotten friend.' After which he snatched his hat and fled, vowing never to return. But this kind of quarrel never lasted long and within a few days he reappeared at our place and resumed the reading of the famous drama. Tears flowed again and in his naïvety Karl Fyodorovitch beseeched us to judge between himself, the public, and his fate, imploring us to take him seriously, as true friends, and not to make fun of him.

One day my mother sent me on an errand to the shop. As I came back, carefully clutching the change in my hands, I met father coming downstairs on his way out. I could not hide my feelings when I saw him and laughed; as he bent down to kiss me he noticed the money in my hands ... I have forgotten to mention that I was so familiar with his expressions that I could recognize his smallest wish at a glance. When he was sad I was torn with sorrow. The thing that most frequently vexed him was not having any money and therefore being unable to get a drink, a thing that had become a habit with him. Bumping into him on the stairs on this occasion I noticed something unusual going on. His tormented eyes were wandering: at first he failed to notice me, but when he saw the shining coins in my hands he suddenly blushed and, turning pale, stretched out his hand for the money and then instantly withdrew it. It was clear that he was experiencing an inner conflict. In the end he appeared to regain control of himself and told me to go upstairs. He continued to go downstairs for a short way, then stopped abruptly and called to me.

He was extremely confused.

'Listen, Netochka,' he said. 'Give me that money. I'll give it back to you. Eh? You'll give it to papa, won't you? You're a good little girl, Netochka, aren't you?'

I had almost known that this would happen, but my first reaction was fear of mother's anger. My timidity and above all the instinctive shame I felt for my father, and for myself, prevented me from handing him the money. He was quick to notice this and hastily added, 'No, it's all right, it's all right . . .'

'No, no, papa, take it. I'll say that I lost it, that the children next door stole it from me.'

'Oh very well then, very well. You see, I always knew you were a clever girl,' he said, his lips quivering. He smiled at me, no longer trying to conceal his delight at feeling the money between his hands. 'You are a good little girl. You're my angel. Give me your hand and let me kiss it!'

He took hold of my hand and tried to kiss it, but I quickly withdrew it. Although I was full of compassion I was overwhelmed with shame. I ran upstairs in a sort of panic, abandoning my father without saying goodbye to him. When I entered the room my cheeks were burning and my heart was throbbing with an unpleasant sensation that I had never experienced before. Nevertheless I bravely told mother that I had dropped the money in the snow and had been unable to find it. I expected at least a beating, but nothing happened. Mother was genuinely beside herself with grief; we were desperately poor. She started to shout at me and then, changing her mind, stopped scolding me and started telling me what a careless and clumsy girl I was and that obviously I did not love her much if I could be so negligent with her money. This observation hurt me more than any beating would have done. But my mother knew me well. She had noticed my sensitivity, which frequently reached a state of morbid irrationality, and she knew well that reproaching me for lack of love would make a deeper impression on me and might make me more careful in the future.

At dusk, at the time when father was expected home, I went downstairs as usual to wait for him. This time I was in a terrible state of mind. My feelings were in a whirl because of something that was causing me agonizing pangs of conscience. I was overjoyed when father arrived; I had an idea that it would help me feel better. He was already slightly elated, but on seeing me he immediately looked troubled and bewildered. He took me off into a corner and, looking nervously towards our door, took the cake he had bought out of his pocket and whispered to me. He told me that I must never take money again or hide it from mother because it was a bad and shameful thing to do. He explained that on this occasion he had needed the money very much but that he would return it and I could say that I had found it again. He repeated that it was shameful to steal from mother and that I must not think of doing it again. He promised that if I obeyed him he would buy me more cake. Finally he added that I ought to feel sympathy for my mother, who was so sick and poor yet still took care of us. I listened to him in terror, my whole body trembling and my eyes brimming with tears. I was so astonished that I could not utter a word or move an inch. After telling me not to cry and not to mention a word to mother, he went into the room. I could see that he himself was embarrassed. I felt panic-stricken and for the rest of the evening I did not dare to look at him or go near him. He too avoided my eyes. Mother was in a dream, pacing the room and mumbling to herself as usual. I think she had had some kind of an attack and was feeling worse. My inner sufferings made me feverish and I could not sleep that night. I was tormented by morbid nightmares. When I could bear it no longer I started weeping bitterly. My mother was awakened by my sobs and called over to me, asking what the matter was. Instead of answering I cried even louder. Then she lit a candle, came over to me and, imagining that I was having a bad dream, she began soothing me.

'Oh, you foolish child!' she said. 'Still crying over dreams at your age. Come on, enough now!'

She kissed me and told me to come and sleep in her bed. But I did not want to; I was too afraid to hug her. My heart was unbelievably troubled and I longed to tell her about it. I was on the verge of telling her but I remembered my father's warning.

'Oh, Netochka, you poor little thing,' said my mother, tucking me into bed and wrapping her cloak around me because she saw that I was shivering and feverishly delirious. 'You'll make yourself ill, like me,' and she gazed mournfully at me. I could not bear to look at her and turned away, shutting my eyes. I do not remember how I fell asleep. I lay for a long time dozing, listening to my mother as she lulled me asleep. I had never before suffered such excruciating torment and heartbreak.

I felt better the following morning. I talked to father without mentioning what had happened the previous day, which I hoped would please him. He had been frowning incessantly but soon cheered up at this. A sort of joy, a childish satisfaction at my carefree attitude came over him. My mother went out before long and then he could restrain himself no longer. He kissed me until I reached a kind of hysterical ecstasy, laughing and crying at the same time. Then he said that I was such a good and clever little girl that he wanted to show me something very special and beautiful. Unbuttoning his waistcoat, he took out the key that hung around his neck on a piece of black string and looked mysteriously into my eyes as if searching for the pleasure he expected me to be feeling. Then he opened the trunk with the key and took out something I had never seen before. He picked up the case with the utmost care and I saw his face transformed. There was no more laughter in his eyes, his face was solemn and triumphant. Using the key, he opened the mysterious box and took out something quite unfamiliar to me, a strangely shaped object. Holding it carefully and reverently in his hands, he told me that this was his violin, his instrument. He said a lot more in a solemn voice, but I did not understand his words and only picked up the phrases I already knew: that he was an artist and a genius, that one day he would be a performer and we would be rich and happy. Tears poured down my cheeks. I was very moved. At last he kissed his violin and then handed it to me to kiss. Seeing that I wanted to look at it more carefully, he led me over to mother's bed and handed me the violin. But I could see that he was terrified that I might break it. I took the violin in my hands and touched the strings which gave forth a faint sound.

'It's music,' I said, looking at father.

'Yes, yes, it's music,' he repeated, rubbing his hands together joyfully. 'You are a clever child, a good child!'

But despite his praise and delight I knew that he was nervous about his violin. I too was a little frightened and hastily gave it back to him. He carefully replaced it in its case, locked it and put the case in the chest. Father stroked me on the head again and promised that every time I behaved as a good, clever and obedient girl he would show me his violin. Thus the violin came to offer mutual consolation. Not until that evening, when he was going out, did father whisper to me that I must not forget what he had said the previous day.

This was the way in which I grew up in our attic room; little by little my love, or perhaps I should say my passion (for I do not know a word strong enough to express fully my overwhelming, anguished feelings for my father), reached a kind of morbid anxiety. I had only one true pleasure, which was dreaming and thinking about him. I had only one true desire, which was to do anything that might please him. How many times did I stand on the stairs waiting for him to come in, often shivering and blue with cold, simply in the hope of catching sight of him one second sooner? I used to become almost delirious with joy whenever he offered me the slightest caress. At the same time I was often dreadfully distressed that I was so obstinately cold towards my poor mother, and at moments I was torn to shreds with pity and misery as I looked at her. I could not be indifferent to their everlasting hostility and I had to choose between them. I had to side with one or the other and I took the side of the half-crazy man because he seemed to me so pitiful, so humiliated, and because he aroused my fantasy. But who knows? Perhaps I attached myself to him because he was so strange, even in appearance, or because he was less gloomy and morbid than my mother; or because he was almost mad and acted the buffoon like a child; or, most probably, because I was less afraid of him and indeed had less respect for him than for my mother. In a way he was nearer my own level. I gradually felt I was rising above him, that I could dominate him a little and that he needed me. I was inwardly proud of this, I gloried in it and, realizing how necessary I was to him, I even played with him at times. I admit that this strange devotion developed into quite a romance ... But it was destined to be shortlived: not long afterwards I lost both my father and my mother. Their life ended in the most terrible catastrophe which still haunts my memory. This is what happened.

CHAPTER THREE

Everyone in Petersburg was excited by a piece of extraordinary news. A rumour was going around concerning the imminent arrival of the famous S., and the entire musical world was astir. Singers, actors, poets, artists, music-lovers and even those who were not at all musical, and boasted of not knowing one note from the next, were rushing with avid enthusiasm to buy tickets. The hall could not seat one-tenth of the aficionados who could afford twenty-five roubles for a ticket. The European fame awarded to S., his old age crowned with laurels, the lasting freshness of his talent, the rumours that in the last few years he had rarely taken up his bow in public, and the certainty that this would be his last European tour before retirement – all contributed to the effect. In short, the sensation caused by the news was profound.

I have already mentioned that the arrival of any new violinist, of any celebrity with the least claim to fame, had a most unpleasant effect on my father. He was always one of the first to rush off and hear the new arrival in order to find out quickly the extent of his merit. He often became ill as a result of the applause that resounded around the newcomer and was only calmed when he managed to discover defects in the violinist's playing. He would then do all he could to circulate his opinion. The poor madman really believed that there was only one musical genius in the whole world and that genius was, of course, himself. The news of the anticipated arrival of a musician as distinguished as S. had a devastating effect on him. I ought to mention that during the past ten years Petersburg had not heard a single performer of S.'s calibre, and consequently my father had no notion of first-rate European artists.

I was told that at the first mention of S.'s visit my father was again to be seen backstage at the theatre. Apparently he was

49

terribly agitated and made uneasy inquiries concerning S. and his forthcoming concert. He had not been seen in the theatre for some time, and his appearance created quite a sensation. Evidently wishing to provoke him, someone challenged him: 'Now, my dear Egor Petrovitch, you can listen to something very different from ballet music, something that will make your life not worth living!' They said he turned pale at this insult, and replied with a frenzied smile: 'We shall see. All that glitters is not gold. S. has only been in Paris, where the French have made a fuss of him, and we all know the French!'

Everyone around him began to laugh. The poor man was offended but, restraining himself, added that he had no more to say on the matter, and that they should wait for the day after tomorrow, when all would be known.

B. told me that just before dusk that evening he met Prince X., a well-known dilettante and a man with a deep understanding and love of the arts. As they were walking along together discussing the newly arrived artist, they caught sight of my father standing on a street corner, gazing intently at a placard in a shop window. The placard announced in large letters the concert to be given by S.

'Do you see that man?' asked B., pointing to my father.

'Who is he?' asked the Prince.

'You've already heard of him. It's Efimov, of whom I have spoken to you more than once and to whom you extended your patronage at one time.'

'Oh, that curious fellow!' said the Prince. 'You've spoken a great deal about him. I hear that he's fascinating. I should like to hear him.'

'It's not worth it,' answered B. 'It's very distressing. I don't know about you, but I find it heartbreaking. His life is a ghastly, hideous tragedy. I feel deeply for him and, no matter how unsociable he's become, I can't help feeling sorry for him. You say, Prince, that he's an interesting fellow. That may well be true, but he creates a most painful impression. In the first place, he's mad, and in the second, he's guilty of three crimes, for he's ruined his wife's and his daughter's lives as well as his own. I know him. It would kill him instantly if he realized what he's done, and the worst part is that for eight years now he's almost realized it, for eight years he's been struggling with his conscience in order to grasp it fully.'

'Did you say he's poor?'

'Yes. But nowadays poverty is almost his happiness: it provides him with an excuse. He can now convince everyone that it's only poverty that has hindered him, and that if he had been rich, free of troubles and had had plenty of free time, we would all have recognized him for the artist he is. He married with the peculiar idea that his wife's thousand roubles would be likely to set him on his feet. He behaved like a visionary and a poet. That is the way he has acted all his life. Do you know what he's been saying for the last eight years? He's been insisting that his wife is the cause of his poverty, and yet he just sits there doing nothing, and won't work. If you were to deprive him of his wife he would be the most miserable creature in existence. It must be several years now since he has touched his violin – and do you know why? Because every time he does he's forced to realize that he's nothing, a nobody, not one bit of an artist. But at least when he's put his violin aside, as now, he can sustain the remote hope that it isn't true. He's a dreamer, he imagines that all of a sudden, at the wave of a wand, he'll become the most famous person in the world. His motto is "*Aut Caesar, aut nihil*", as if one could become Caesar just like that. He thirsts for fame. But if such feeling becomes the main source of an artist's activity then he ceases to be an artist, for he has lost the artist's chief instinct, which must be to love art simply because it is art, and not for its rewards. Whereas it's quite the opposite with S. When he takes up his bow, nothing in the world exists for him except music. After his violin comes money, and fame comes third. But he doesn't worry himself much over that ... Do you know what it is that's bothering that pitiful man at the moment?' continued B., referring to Efimov. 'He's obsessed by the most unimaginably stupid and pathetic question, namely, whether he's superior to S. or vice versa, nothing less. He's still convinced that he's the world's leading musician. Prove to him that he's not a musical genius and I assure you he'd die on the spot, thunderstruck. It must be terrible to part with a fixed idea to which one's whole life has been dedicated, and which rests on genuine foundations, for he had a true vocation at first.'

'It will be interesting to see what becomes of him when he hears S.,' observed Prince X.

'Yes,' said B. thoughtfully. 'But no, he'll recover at once. His madness is stronger than the truth and he'll quickly invent some counter-argument.'

'Do you think so?' rejoined the Prince.

At this point they found themselves drawing level with my father. He was trying to pass them unnoticed, but B. stopped him and began speaking to him. He asked whether he would be at S.'s concert. My father answered in an indifferent tone, saying he did not know, that he had certain matters at hand that were more important than any concert or passing virtuoso. He said he might, however, consider it, but would have to wait and see whether he had a couple of free hours, and if he did he might as well go. Then he glanced swiftly at B. and Prince X., smiled mistrustfully and, snatching at his hat, nodded and walked off, saying he was in a hurry.

I had spotted my father's anxiety the previous day. I was not sure exactly what it was that was troubling him, but I noticed that he was in a state of desperate agitation. Even my mother had noticed it, although she was very ill at the time and barely able to leave her bed. Father had been continually going out and coming back in. In the morning three or four visitors, old theatre companions, had been to see him. This surprised me as, apart from Karl Petrovitch, no one had been to see us since he had left the theatre. Then in came Karl Petrovitch, panting and carrying a poster. I listened and watched attentively; I was troubled, feeling as if I alone were responsible for all the anxiety and commotion written across my father's face. I was keen to understand what they were saying, and I heard the name S. for the first time. Then I realized that it cost at least fifteen roubles to see S. I also remember hearing my father say, with a wave of the hand, that he knew all these foreign wonders, these unheard-of talents, including S., and that they were all Jews, trying to get hold of Russian money because the Russians, in all their simplicity, would believe any nonsense, especially anything the French made a fuss about. I was already familiar with the word 'untalented'. And then the guests left, leaving father in very low spirits. I saw that for some reason he was angry with S., and in order to cheer him up and regain his favour I went over to the table, picked up the poster and, spelling it out aloud, pronounced the name S. Then, laughing and looking round at father, who was sitting in his chair, deep in thought, I said: 'I expect that he is like Karl Fyodorovitch and will never make it either.'

Father started, as if with fright, and snatched the poster from my hands. Stamping his feet and shouting at me, he grabbed his hat and headed for the door. Then he suddenly turned round and beckoned me into the passage, where he started to kiss me, telling me that I was a clever child, that he did not believe I really wanted to upset him and that he was expecting a huge favour from me, but he could not say exactly what it was. I found it painful to listen to him; I knew that his words and endearments were insincere and it had a shattering effect on me. I started to worry about him.

At dinner the following day – the day before the concert – father appeared to be completely crushed. He was quite changed and kept looking at me and my mother. In the end, much to my surprise, he started talking to my mother (to my surprise because he rarely spoke to her). After dinner he began making a fuss of me, calling me out into the passage every few minutes on one pretext or another. He kept beckoning me, looking around as if afraid of being caught, patting me on the head, telling me what a good and obedient child I was and how he was sure I loved him enough to do what he was about to ask of me. It all became very oppressive and it was not until he called me out for about the tenth time that I finally realized what was going on. Looking around nervously, he asked me whether I knew where mother had put the twenty-five roubles that she had brought home the day before. I froze with horror as I heard this question, but just at that moment there was a noise on the stairs and father, alarmed, pushed me aside and ran out. Towards evening he returned, distraught and gloomy. He sat in his chair in silence, casting nervous looks at me from time to time. I was overwhelmed with dread and intentionally avoided his eyes. Eventually my mother, who had been in bed all day, called to me, gave me some coins and asked me to go out and buy her some tea and some sugar. We very seldom drank tea in our family, and it was only when she felt particularly ill and feverish that mother allowed herself to indulge in what was a luxury to people of our means. I took the money, went out and started running, afraid of being chased. It was exactly as I feared: my father caught up with me in the street and led me back to the foot of the stairs.

'Netochka,' he began in a trembling voice, 'my little darling! Listen, give me that money and tomorrow . . .'

'Papa, Papa!' I cried, falling on to my knees and imploring him. 'Papa, I can't! It's impossible. Mama needs the tea. I can't steal from her, really I can't. I'll do it for you another time.'

'So, you don't want to? You don't want to?' he whispered in a frenzy. 'It means you don't love me, eh? All right! I'll leave you now. You can stay with Mama. I'm going away and I'll leave you behind. Do you hear me, you wicked girl, do you hear me?'

'Oh Papa!' I screamed, utterly horrified. 'Take the money, there! Now what shall I do?' I said, wringing my hands and tugging his coat-tails. 'Mama will cry, and she'll scold me again.'

He had clearly not expected this kind of resistance, but in the end he took the money and, weary of my sobs and whines, he left me on the stairs as he rushed outside. I went back upstairs, but lost my nerve on reaching the door to our room: I could not, I dared not enter. Everything inside me felt rebellious and wounded. I covered my face with my hands and rushed over to the window, as I had done the first time I heard my father speak of his wish to see my mother dead. I was in a sort of stupor, rooted to the spot and shaking all over as I waited, listening to every sound on the stairs. At last I heard someone coming rapidly upstairs. It was him; I recognized his tread.

'Are you there?' he asked in a whisper. I rushed over to him.

'There!' he said, thrusting the money into my hands. 'There!

Take it back. I'm not your father, do you hear me? I don't wish to be your father. You love your mother more than me! So, go to mother! But I don't want to have anything to do with you!'

As he said this he pushed me aside and ran downstairs again. I ran after him in floods of tears.

'Papa, dearest Papa, I will obey you,' I cried. 'I do love you more than mother. Take the money back, take it!' But he did not hear me; he had vanished. All that evening I felt crushed, and shook feverishly. I remember mother saying something to me, calling me, but I was hardly conscious and was unable to see or hear anything. In the end I went into a fit; I began screaming and crying. Mother was frightened and did not know what to do. She picked me up and took me over to her bed. Somehow, I do not remember how, I fell asleep with my arms around her neck, trembling and shaking all over. The whole night passed in this way. I woke up very late the next morning and found that mother was no longer in the room. She often went out to do things at that time of the day. A stranger had come to see father, and they were talking noisily together. I forced myself to wait until the visitor had left and then, once we were alone, I rushed over to father, sobbing and begging him to forgive me for what had happened the previous day.

'And will you be a clever little girl like before?' he asked me sternly.

'I will, Papa, yes I will,' I answered. 'I'll tell you where mother keeps her money. She keeps it in that little box, it was there in that box yesterday.'

'Keeps it? Where? Where does she keep it?' he cried, jumping up from his chair. 'Where does she keep it?'

'It's locked up, father,' I said. 'Wait a bit, wait until the evening when Mama goes to get change; I know she's run out.'

'I must have fifteen roubles, Netochka, do you hear? Just fifteen roubles! Get it for me today and I'll return it tomorrow. And I'll go straight away and buy you some sweets and some nuts ... And I'll buy you a doll too ... and again tomorrow. Yes, I will bring you sweets every day if you're a good girl.'

'You needn't, Papa, you needn't. I don't want sweets. I won't eat them, I'll give them back to you!' I cried, choking with tears and feeling as if my heart would burst. I felt at that moment that he was not really feeling sorry for me and that he neither loved me nor realized how much I loved him if he thought that I would do whatever he wanted just for sweets. I, the child, understood him thoroughly and I felt as if that understanding had wounded me for ever. I did not believe that I could love him as before and I feared that I had lost my former Papa. He was in a kind of ecstasy as a result of my promise. He knew that I was prepared to do anything for him, and God knows how much that 'anything' meant to me. I knew how important the money was to mother, and I knew that she might become ill through the distress of losing it. But he saw nothing. He treated me like a three-year-old child, whereas in fact I understood everything. His delight knew no bounds. He kissed me, begged me not to cry and promised that we would leave mother and go away together that very day, intending, I suppose, to flatter my eternal daydream. He took a poster out of his pocket and began assuring me that the man he was going to see today was his enemy, his mortal enemy, but that his enemies never succeeded. As he talked to me about his enemies he seemed just like a child himself. He noticed that I was not smiling in my usual way and that I was listening to him in silence. He took his hat and hurried out of the room. Before leaving he kissed me, nodding his head in a half-smile as if uncertain that he could trust me not to change my mind.

I have already said that he was like a madman, and this had been apparent since the day before. He needed the money to buy a ticket for the concert, which he believed would resolve everything. He seemed to have a premonition that this concert would decide his fate, but he was so distracted that the previous day he had wanted to take a few copecks from me, as if that would buy his ticket. He became like a stranger during dinner. He simply could not sit still and he did not touch any of his food. He kept getting up from his chair and then sitting down again as though he were hesitating over something. At one moment he would snatch up his hat as if going off somewhere, then at another he would become strangely absent, whispering to himself, then suddenly glancing at me, winking as if to say that he wanted the money as soon as possible, and was annoyed because I had not obtained it already. Even my mother noticed his strange behaviour, and she looked at him in bewilderment. I felt as if I were under sentence of death. When the meal was over I huddled in a corner, shivering constantly and counting each second as I waited for mother to send me out to buy something. I have never spent more agonizing hours in my life, and I shall never forget them. God knows the feelings I experienced! There are moments when you go through more in your inner consciousness than in a whole lifetime. I felt that I was doing something very wicked. He himself had prompted my better instincts, when, like a coward, he had pushed me into wrongdoing for the first time. Frightened by it himself, he had explained to me that I had done something wrong. Surely he must have understood how hard it is to deceive someone of my temperament; someone who already, at an exceptionally early age, had experienced and comprehended so much good and evil. I did, of course, understand that it was through sheer desperation that he was prompted to lead me again and again into sin, sacrificing my defenceless childhood and running the risk of disturbing still further my unstable mind. And now, huddled in my corner, I wondered why he promised me rewards for something I had made up my mind to do of my own free will. New sensations, yearnings, and doubts all crowded my mind, tormenting my thoughts. Then all at once I began thinking about mother; I imagined her grief at the loss of her last copecks. Finally she put aside her work, exhausted, and called for me. I was trembling all over as I went to see her. She had taken some money out of the drawer and gave it to me, saying: 'Run along now, Netochka. Only, please God, don't let them give you short change as they did the other day. And don't lose it.'

I glanced at my father with an imploring expression, but he only nodded and smiled at me encouragingly, as he wrung his hands impatiently. The clock struck six; the concert was due to start at seven. He, too, was going through a lot during those hours of suspense.

I stopped on the stairs and waited for father. He was so excited and agitated that, without any attempt at concealment, he dashed out after me. I handed him the money. It was dark on the staircase; I could not see his face properly, but I could feel the way he quivered all over as he took it from me. I stood there stunned, unable to move. I only came to my senses when he sent me back upstairs to fetch his hat.

'Papa! ... Surely ... aren't you coming with me?' I said in a broken voice, thinking that my only hope was that he would intercede for me.

'No, you'd better go alone, all right? No, wait! Wait!' he cried, suddenly remembering something. 'Wait a minute. I'll get you something nice in just a minute, but first go in and bring me my hat.' I felt as if an icy hand was gripping my heart. Screaming, I pushed him from me and ran upstairs. My face filled with horror as I entered the room, and if I had told my mother that I had been robbed of the money she surely would have believed me. But I could say nothing at that moment. In a convulsive fit of grief I threw myself on to my mother's bed and hid my face in my hands. A minute later, the door creaked open and my father timidly entered. He had come for his hat.

'Where's the money?' cried my mother, guessing that something was up. 'Where's the money? Tell me, tell me!' She snatched me up from the bed and made me stand in the middle of the room.

I stood in silence with my eyes on the floor. I was barely able to understand what was happening to me, or what they were doing.

'Where's the money?' she cried once again, turning abruptly from me to my father, who had grabbed his hat. 'Where's the money?' she repeated. 'Ah, so she's given it to you, the godless creature! You murderer! Curse of my life! Do you want to ruin her too? A child! Here! Here! No, no, you won't get away with it!'

In a flash she flew to the door, locked it from the inside and took the key.

'Speak! Confess!' she said to me, in a voice scarcely audible from emotion. 'Tell me everything! Speak, speak, or I don't know what I'll do to you.' She grabbed my hands and squeezed them as she interrogated me. I vowed at that moment to keep silent and not say a word about father. I raised my eyes timidly at him for the last time ... One look, one word from him expressing what I was hoping and praying for and I should have been happy, in spite of my suffering and torment ... But, my God! With a cruel, threatening gesture he ordered me to be silent, as if I could have been intimidated any further at that moment! There was a lump in my throat, I could not breathe and fell senseless on the floor ... I had an attack of nerves, as on the previous day.

I came to my senses at the sound of someone knocking at the door. When mother opened it I saw a man dressed in livery, who looked at us all in bewilderment as he entered, asking for the musician Efimov. My stepfather introduced himself. The footman gave him a note and announced that he had come from B., who at that moment was with Prince X. In the envelope was a complimentary ticket to S.'s concert.

The appearance of the footman in his sumptuous livery, presenting himself as one of the Prince's staff sent expressly to see the poor musician Efimov, instantly made a tremendous impression on my mother. I have already mentioned, when describing her character, that she, poor woman, still loved my father. And now, in spite of eight years of never-ending misery and suffering, her heart remained the same: she could still love him! Who knows ... perhaps at this moment she envisaged a complete change in his fortunes. Even the faintest glimmer of hope influenced her ... perhaps she too was a little bit affected by her crazy husband's unwavering self-assurance! Indeed, it would have been remarkable if this self-assurance had not had some effect on her, for she was a weak woman. The consideration shown by Prince X. spurred her into concocting a thousand and one plans for her husband. In an instant she was prepared to reconcile herself to him, to forgive him for what he had done to her life and even to overlook his last crime, the sacrifice of her only child. In a burst of renewed enthusiasm and hope, she could reduce the crime to a mere shortcoming, to an act of cowardice induced by poverty, the degradation of his life and his desperate situation. She was so impulsive that at that moment she was again capable of forgiveness and infinite compassion for her ruined husband.

59

My father was bustling about; he too was impressed by the attention of Prince X. and of B. He turned straight away to mother, whispered something to her and she left the room. She came back two minutes later with some small change, then father immediately gave a silver rouble to the messenger, who left with a polite bow. Mother again left the room and returned with an iron. She fetched her husband's best frock-coat and began pressing it. She herself tied the white cambric cravat around his neck. It had been preserved, on the off-chance of being used, in the wardrobe and forgotten long ago, together with his black, and by now very shabby, dress-coat, which had been made for him when he entered the service of the theatre orchestra. Having completed his toilet, father took his hat, and was on the point of going when he asked for a glass of water; he was pale, and he sat down on a chair feeling faint. It was I who gave him the water; perhaps the feeling of hostility had crept into mother's heart again and cooled her original enthusiasm.

Father left, and we were alone. I crouched in the corner and watched my mother, silently, for a long time. I had never before seen her so excited. Her lips were trembling and her ashen face suddenly glowed; from time to time her whole body shook. At last her grief came pouring out in stifled sobs, complaints and lamentations.

'It's me, it's me who's to blame for everything, miserable woman that I am!' she said to herself. 'What will become of her? What will become of her when I die?' She stood motionless in the middle of the room as though stricken with horror by the thought. 'Netochka, my child! My poor darling . . . my poor unhappy child!' she said, taking me by the hand and kissing me convulsively. 'Who will take care of you when I'm gone, when even now I can't educate you, look after you and care for you as I should? Ah, don't you understand me? Do you understand? Will you remember what I've just said to you, Netochka? Will you remember this in future?'

'I will, mother, I will,' I said, clasping my hands and beseeching her. She held me for a long time in a warm embrace, as if terrified of the thought of parting from me. My heart was bursting.

'Mama, Mama,' I said, sobbing, 'why don't you ... why don't you love Papa?' My sobs prevented me from finishing what I was saying. A groan burst forth from her bosom, and in another rush of acute misery she began pacing the room.

'My poor, poor child! And I never noticed how she was growing up. She knows everything, she knows everything! My God! What sort of ideas we've given her, what an example!' And again she wrung her hands in despair. She came over to me and, with a frantic display of love, tears streaming down her face, she kissed me and begged my forgiveness. I have never seen so much suffering ... Finally, exhausted, she dropped off into a doze. An hour passed and then she got up, still weary, and told me to go to sleep. I went off into my corner and wrapped myself in a blanket, but I could not sleep. I was worried both about her and about father, whose return I was impatiently awaiting, terrified at the thought of it. After half an hour mother came over, holding a candle, to see whether I was asleep. After looking at me she went, very quietly, to the cupboard, opened it and poured herself a glass of wine. She drank it and went to sleep, leaving the candle burning on the table and the door unlocked, as she always did when father was expected back late.

I lay there in a state of semi-consciousness, but sleep would not come to my eyes. As soon as I had closed them I would wake up again, trembling from some horrible dream. My misery grew worse and worse. I wanted to scream, but the scream remained unuttered. At last, late in the night, I heard the door open. I do not remember how much time went by, but when I opened my eyes I saw father. He seemed dreadfully pale. He was sitting in a chair beside the door, lost in thought. A deathly silence filled the room. The flickering candle cast a gloomy light on our hovel.

I watched father for a long time but still he did not stir; he remained in the same motionless position with his head bowed and his hands pressed rigidly against his knees. Several times I tried to call him but could not. I was still in a numbed stupor. Then suddenly he roused himself, raised his head and got up from the chair. For some minutes he stood in the centre of the room as if trying to make some decision. Then he quickly moved

61

over to mother's bed, listened to make sure she was sleeping and went over to the chest where he kept the violin. He unlocked the chest, took out the black case and put it on the table, looking round again. His eyes had a furtive, wandering look such as I had never seen before.

He was picking up the violin when he broke off in order to lock the door. Then, noticing the open cupboard, he went stealthily over to it, caught sight of the glass and the wine, poured some and drank it. Then for the third time he took up the violin, but for the third time put it down and went to mother's bed. Frozen in fear, I watched to see what would happen.

He stood listening for a very long time, then, putting the quilt over her face, he began feeling her with his hand. I started. He bent down again, almost putting his head against hers. When he got up for the last time there seemed to be a smile flickering over his horribly pale face. Silently and carefully he pulled up the blanket and covered the sleeping woman; he covered her head, her feet . . . I began shaking with a terror I did not understand. I felt frightened for mother; I was frightened by her deep sleep and I looked uneasily at the still, sharp outline of her limbs underneath the quilt . . . A terrible thought flashed like lightning across my mind.

Having completed the preparations, father went back to the cupboard and started drinking the remaining wine. His body trembled as he walked to the table. His face was pale beyond all recognition. He picked up the violin again. I knew what it was now, but I was expecting something awful, hideous, monstrous . . . I shuddered at the first sound of the notes. Father had begun to play. The sounds came out jerkily; he kept stopping abruptly as if remembering something; eventually, with a distraught, agonized expression, he put down his bow and gave a strange look in the direction of the bed, before going over to it again . . . I did not miss a single movement he made and watched him, petrified.

Suddenly he began hurriedly groping for something, and again the same ghastly thought went through me like lightning. I wondered why mother was sleeping so soundly. How was it that she did not wake up when he touched her face with his hand? At last, I saw him gathering all the clothes he could find. He took mother's pelisse, his old frock-coat, his dressing-gown, even the clothes I had taken off for bed. He threw them all in a pile covering her. She lay completely motionless, not a limb stirring.

She was sleeping very soundly!

Father seemed to breathe more freely once he had finished his task. This time nothing hindered him, but all the same he was troubled by something. Moving the candle, he stood with his face towards the door, avoiding the bed. Eventually he took the violin and, with a gesture of despair, drew the bow across it ... The music began.

But it was not music ... I remember everything distinctly; to the end I can remember everything that caught my attention. No, this was not like the music I later came to hear. They were not the notes of the violin, but the sound of a terrible voice that was resounding through our room for the first time. Either my impressions were incorrect or delirious, or else my senses were so thrown by all that I had witnessed that they were prepared for frightful, agonizing impressions – but I am firmly convinced that I heard groans, the cries of a human voice. Complete despair flowed forth in these chords and when, at the end, there resounded the last awful note, in which was expressed all that is terrible in a cry, the agony of torture and the misery of hopelessness, I could bear it no longer. I began trembling, tears poured from my eyes, and I rushed over to father with a terrified shriek and grabbed him by the hand. He cried out and put down his violin.

He stood for a moment, stunned, then his eyes lit up and darted around the room. He seemed to be looking for something; suddenly he snatched up his violin, waved it over my head, and ... another minute and he might have killed me on the spot.

'Papa!' I shouted to him. 'Papa!'

He shook like a leaf when he heard my voice, and took a couple of steps backwards.

'Oh, so there's still you! It's not over yet! So you're still left with me!' he shouted, lifting me above his shoulders, into the air.

'Papa!' I cried again. 'For God's sake, don't frighten me so! I'm scared! Ah!' My cries impressed him; he put me down on the ground gently and looked at me without speaking for a while, as if recognizing and remembering something. Then he changed abruptly, as some ghastly thought ran through him. Tears welled up in his dulled eyes, and he leaned down, looking intently into my face.

'Papa,' I said, riddled with fear, 'don't look at me in that way! Papa! Let's go away from here! Quick, let's go! Let's run away!'

'Yes, we'll run away, it's high time. Come along, Netochka, hurry, hurry!' And he rushed about as if only just realizing what he had to do. He looked around and, catching sight of mother's handkerchief on the floor, picked it up and put it in his pocket. Then he saw her bonnet and picked that up too, as if he were preparing for a long journey, gathering together all the things he might want. I swiftly put on my clothes, and then started snatching up all the things I thought were necessary for the journey.

'Is everything ready, everything?' my father asked. 'Is everything ready? Hurry now, hurry!'

I quickly tied up my bundle, threw a kerchief over my head, and we were about to depart, when it suddenly occurred to me that I must take the picture hanging on the wall. Father immediately agreed to this.

'Quiet now.' He spoke in a whisper, urging me to be quick. The picture was hanging high on the wall. The two of us fetched a chair, put a stool on it, clambered up and, after prolonged effort, took it down. At last everything was ready for our journey. He took me by the hand and again we were about to depart when father suddenly stopped me. He scratched his forehead for a long time as though there were something he had forgotten to do. Finally he seemed to find what it was, and searched for the key which was under mother's pillow, then rummaged hurriedly through the chest of drawers. At last he came back to me, holding some money which he had found in the box.

'Here, take this,' he whispered to me. 'Don't lose it, remember, you must remember!' At first he put the money in my hand,

then took it back and thrust it in the top of my dress. I re-
member shuddering when I felt the silver against my body, and
I think it was then that I first understood the meaning of money.
We were ready once more, but again he suddenly stopped me.

'Netochka,' he said, as if gathering strength. 'My little child, I
have forgotten . . . What is it? . . . What do we need? . . . I can't
remember . . . Yes, yes, I've got it, I remember! . . . Come here
Netochka!'

He took me over to the corner where the icon stood and told
me to kneel down.

'Pray, my child, pray! You'll feel better! . . . Yes, really, it'll
make you better,' he whispered, pointing to the icon and looking at
me rather strangely. 'Say your prayers,' he said in an imploring
voice.

I went down on my knees and clasped my hands. I was once
more filled with horror and despair, which completely overwhelmed me. I sank to the floor where I lay for some minutes
like a dying person. I concentrated all my thoughts and feelings
in prayer, but was overcome with fear. I got up exhausted with
anguish. I no longer wished to go with him; I was afraid of him
and I wanted to stay where I was. At last the thought that was
tormenting and torturing me burst forth: 'Papa,' I said, breaking
into tears, 'what about Mama? . . . What's the matter with
Mama? Where is she? Where is my Mama?'

I could not go on – my face was flooded with tears.

He, too, was in tears as he looked at me. Taking me by the
hand, he led me over to the corner of the bed, threw aside the
heap of clothing and pulled back the blankets. My God! There
she was, lying there dead, already cold and blue. I flung myself
frantically on top of her and embraced her corpse. Father pushed
me on to my knees.

'Bow down to her, child!' he said. 'Say goodbye to her . . .' I
bowed down. My father knelt beside me. He was horribly pale,
his lips quivered and he was whispering something: *It wasn't
me, Netochka, it wasn't me.* He pointed at the dead body with a
trembling finger. *Do you hear? It wasn't me, I'm not guilty of this.
Remember, Netochka.*

'Papa, let's go,' I whispered in terror. 'It's time!'

'Yes, it is time now, we should have left long ago,' he said, gripping me tightly by the hand and making to leave the room. 'Now, let's be off. Thank God, thank God it's all over now!' We went downstairs. The sleepy porter looked at us with suspicion as he unlocked the gate. Father, perhaps afraid of him, ran ahead through the gate, leaving me to catch up with him. We went down our street and came out on the bank of the canal. Snow had fallen on the pavements during the night and was now coming down in tiny flakes. It was cold; I was chilled to the bone and ran along beside father, clutching his coat-tails fitfully. His violin was under his arm, and he was continually stopping to hitch it up.

We had been walking for a quarter of an hour when at last he turned along a sloping pavement which led down to the edge of the canal and sat down at the end of the kerbstone. Two steps away from us was a hole cut in the ice. There was not a soul in sight. Oh, God! How well I still remember the terrible feeling that overpowered me! At last everything that I had been dreaming of for a whole year had come true. We had left our miserable lodgings. But was this what I was expecting, was it this I had dreamt of, was this what I had created in my childish fantasy when I conjured up the happiness of the man whom I loved in such an unchildish way? At that moment it was, above all, the thought of my mother that tortured me the most. Why, I wondered, had we left her alone? Why had we abandoned her body like some useless object? I remember it was this that particularly troubled me.

'Papa,' I began, unable to bear the strain of my worry for her, 'Papa!'

'What is it?' he said sullenly.

'Why have we left Mama there, Papa? Why have we abandoned her?' I asked, bursting into tears. 'Papa, let's go home again. Let's fetch someone for her.'

'Yes, yes,' he exclaimed, and with a start he sprang up from the kerbstone as if suddenly struck by a solution to all his problems. 'Yes, Netochka, it's no use. You must go back to mother, she's getting cold there! Go back to her, Netochka, go! It isn't dark, there's a candle there, don't be afraid. Fetch someone for her and then come back to me. You go alone and I'll be waiting here ... I won't go away.'

I set off at once, but had scarcely reached the pavement when something suddenly seemed to stab me in the heart ... I looked round and saw that he was already running in the opposite direction ... he was running away from me, leaving me alone, abandoned in a moment! I screamed as loud as I could and, panic-stricken, I rushed to catch up with him. I was gasping for breath, but still he ran faster and faster ... and he disappeared from sight. I stumbled on his hat on the road; it must have been lost in his flight. I picked it up and started running again. I was out of breath and my legs were giving way beneath me. I felt something indescribable was happening to me. I kept thinking it was a dream, and experienced sensations similar to those of my dreams: running away from someone, my legs failing me, and falling unconscious as the pursuer caught up with me. My heart was torn by an agonizing sensation. I felt sorry for him, and it made my heart bleed to think of him running away without an overcoat or a hat – and running away from me, his beloved child ... I wanted to catch up with him, simply to kiss him warmly once more and to tell him not to be afraid of me; to calm him and reassure him that I would not run after him if he did not want me to, but would return to mother alone. At last, I caught sight of him disappearing down a side-street. Running in that direction, I turned down another, and could still make him out in front of me. Then my strength gave out; I began crying and screaming. I remember that during my pursuit I bumped into a couple of passers-by, who had stopped in the middle of the road and were looking at us in amazement.

'Papa, Papa!' I cried for the last time, as I slipped on the pavement and fell at the gates of a house. I could feel my face bathed in blood. A moment later I lost consciousness.

I woke up in a warm, soft bed, greeted by the kind, welcoming faces of people who seemed overjoyed at my recovery. I glimpsed an old lady with spectacles on her nose, a tall man looking at me with sincere compassion, a beautiful young woman and, lastly, a grey-haired old man who was

holding my head and looking at his watch. I had woken to
another existence. One of the people I had bumped into during
my flight was Prince X., and it was at the gate to his house that
I had fallen. When, after long investigations, they discovered
who I was, the Prince (who had sent my father the ticket to S.'s
concert) was struck by the unusual coincidence and decided to
take me into his house and bring me up with his own children.
They tried to find out what had happened to my father, and
learnt that he had been spotted in a fit of raving madness
somewhere on the outskirts of the town and had been taken to
a hospital, where he had died two days later.

He died because such a death was necessary to him, it was a
natural sequel to his life. He was bound to die like that, once all
the things that had supported him in his life had begun to
crumble, fading like a ghost, like an incorporeal and empty
dream. He died when his last hope had vanished, when in one
instant everything with which he had deluded himself and
which had sustained his entire existence disintegrated before
his eyes. The unbearable glow of truth blinded him, and he
recognized falsities for what they were. In his last hour he had
heard an exceptional genius, forcing him to acknowledge his
own worth and thus condemning him for ever. As the last note
soared from the master's violin, the whole mystery of art was
revealed to him and real genius, eternally young, powerful and
true, crushed him. It seemed as if all that had weighed on him
during his life in mysterious, intangible torments; all that had
deluded and tortured him in dreams from which he had fled in
horror, protecting himself with a lie; all that he had had presentiments of, but had been too scared to face – all suddenly
became crystal clear to him, naked to his sight which had, until
then, refused to recognize light for light, darkness for darkness.
The truth was more than his eyes could bear and, seeing for the
first time what had been, what was and what awaited him, he
was blinded as by a lightning stroke. The event he had been
waiting for all his life, with fear and trembling, had suddenly
arrived. There had always been an axe hanging over his head.
All his life he had been tortured by the fear that at any moment
it might fall and strike him. . . At last it fell! The blow was fatal. He

tried to escape the sentence passed on him, but there was nowhere for him to escape; his last hope had vanished, his last pretext had disappeared. The woman who had hampered him for so many years, the woman who had stopped him from living, and with whose death he sought his own resurrection, was now dead. At last he was alone with no one to impede him; he was finally freed! For the last time, in convulsive anguish, he tried to judge himself, to judge himself severely and relentlessly like an impartial critic, but his weakened bow could only feebly repeat the last musical phrase of the genius ... At that instant madness, which had been watching over him for ten years, struck him down once and for all.

CHAPTER FOUR

I slowly regained my health; but even when I was no longer confined to my bed, my brain was still in a sort of stupor, and for a long time I could not understand what exactly had happened to me. There were moments when I thought I was dreaming, and I remember longing to find out that all that had taken place might really turn out to be a dream! Falling asleep at night, I used to hope that I would suddenly wake up and find myself once again in our miserable attic with father and mother ... Eventually my position grew clearer to me, and I gradually understood that I was completely alone and living with strangers. Then, for the first time, I felt an orphan.

I started to look about eagerly at all the new things that were surrounding me. At first everything seemed strange and wonderful; it all confused me: the new faces, new customs, the rooms of the old princely mansion ... I can picture them now: large, high-ceilinged and luxurious, but so grim and gloomy that I remember being afraid of making my way across the long drawing-room, in which I used to feel totally lost. I had not yet completely recovered from my illness, and my thoughts were sombre and gloomy, in perfect harmony with this majestically lugubrious dwelling. Moreover, a melancholy that I did not myself understand was growing stronger and stronger in my young heart. I would stop in wonder before a picture, a mirror, an elaborately carved fireplace, or a statue that seemed to be deliberately hiding in some secluded niche in order to spy on me and frighten me. I would stop and then forget why I had stopped, what I wanted, what I had been thinking about and, recollecting myself, I felt afraid and agitated, my heart beating furiously.

Among those who occasionally came to see how I was when I was lying ill in bed, there was one who, besides the old doctor, impressed me the most. He was quite an elderly man, rather grave, but very kindly in his expression, and he used to look down at me with deep compassion. I liked his face more than any of the others. I longed to speak to him, but was too afraid; he always looked so despondent, spoke so little and so abruptly, and there was never so much as a trace of a smile on his lips. This was Prince X., the man who had found me and in whose house I was being looked after. As I began to get better, his visits became less frequent. On the last visit, he brought me some sweets and a children's picture-book. Then he kissed me, made the sign of the cross over me and begged me to be more cheerful. He comforted me by saying that I should soon have a friend, his daughter Katya, a little girl like myself, who was now in Moscow. He said something to the governess, an elderly Frenchwoman, and to the nanny who was taking care of me, giving them instructions concerning me, and then he left. I did not see him again for three weeks.

The Prince lived in complete solitude in his house. The Princess lived in the larger part of the house, and sometimes she, too, did not see him for weeks on end. Later on, I noticed that none of the members of the household spoke about him much, and they behaved as if he were not there. They all respected him, and one could see that they loved him too, and yet they regarded him as a strange man. It appeared that he himself realized that he was very odd, not quite like other people. He therefore avoided coming into contact with others. Later I will speak of him at greater length and in detail.

One morning they dressed me in fine white linen, put me into a black woollen dress with white collars (on which I gazed with disconsolate wonder), brushed my hair and took me downstairs to the Princess's apartments. I stood petrified when I entered her room; I had never before seen such wealth and grandeur. But it was a fleeting impression, and I went pale when I heard the Princess order that I should be brought closer. Even while they had been dressing me, I had had the feeling that I was being prepared for some ordeal, though God knows what suggested this to me. In truth, I entered into my new life with a strange mistrust of everything around me. But the Princess was very polite to me, and she kissed me. I looked at her a little less nervously. It was the same lovely lady whom I had seen when I first regained consciousness. But I trembled all over when I kissed her and could not summon the strength to answer her questions. She told me to sit down next to her on a low stool, a position I felt had been assigned to me beforehand. I could see that the Princess evidently wanted nothing more than to embrace me heart and soul; to pet me and to take the place of my mother. But I was incapable of appreciating my good fortune and did nothing to impress her. I was given a beautiful picture-book and told to look at it. The Princess was writing a letter, and every now and then she put aside her pen to speak to me again; but I was embarrassed and perplexed, and said nothing sensible. I admit that, although my life had been unusual – and fate, moving in mysterious ways, undoubtedly played an important role – and although there had been much in my life that was interesting, unaccountable and even fantastic, I myself turned out, as if in spite of this melodramatic background, to be a very ordinary child, scared, as it were, crushed, and rather silly. It was this last quality which particularly displeased the Princess, and I think she grew thoroughly tired of me after a short time, for which I had only myself to blame. Between two and three o'clock the visitors began to arrive, and the Princess at once became more attentive and affectionate towards me. In answer to the questions put to her about me, she said it was an extremely interesting story, and began telling it in French. As she recounted it, her visitors looked at me, nodding their heads and exclaiming. One young man eyed me through his *lorgnette*, another grey-haired and perfumed gentleman wanted to kiss me, while in the meantime I sat there with my eyes to the floor, shaking, frightened to move and alternately paling and flushing crimson. My heart ached. My mind turned to the past, to our attic, to father and our long evenings together, and to mother. When I thought of mother tears welled up in my eyes, there was a lump in my throat and I longed to run away, to disappear, to be alone . . . Then, when the visitors had left, the Princess's face became visibly colder. She looked at me crossly, spoke abruptly and frightened me with her piercing black eyes, which she sometimes fixed on me for as long as a quarter of an hour, compressing her narrow lips. I was taken back upstairs in the evening. I fell asleep in a fever, and woke up during the night miserable and crying over my bad dreams. In the morning the whole procedure was repeated, and I was taken to see the Princess again.

Eventually she grew bored of relating my adventures to her visitors, and they were weary of commiserating. Besides, I was such an ordinary child, 'lacking in any *naïveté*', as I recall the Princess saying during a tête-à-tête with a middle-aged lady who asked her if she were not bored with me. And then one evening I was taken away, not to be brought back again. I was no longer shown any favouritism. However, I was allowed to wander around the house freely, wherever I liked. I felt too painfully and miserably morbid to be able to sit still for long, and was very glad to be able to escape from everyone into the large rooms downstairs. I remember that I had a special longing to talk to the servants, but was so afraid of annoying them that I remained alone. My favourite way of passing the time was to retreat to some corner, out of sight, where, hidden behind some piece of furniture, I would start remembering and visualizing all that had happened. But the strange thing was that I seemed to have forgotten what had happened at the very end of the ghastly episode with my parents. There remained only the mental picture to suggest the facts. I did remember it all really: the night, the violin, father. I remembered how I got the money for him, but somehow I could not interpret or explain all that had happened ... Only my heart grew heavier, and when in my memories I came to the episode in which I was praying beside my dead mother, a cold shiver ran down my spine; I trembled, gave a faint cry and with stifled breath and a thumping heart rushed out of my corner in a panic. I was wrong, however, in saying that they left me alone, for I was watched closely and diligently. The Prince's orders were performed with exactitude: he had given instructions that I was to be allowed complete freedom, was not to be restricted in any way, but that I was not to be let out of sight for a moment. I noticed that every so often one of the household would glance into whatever room I was in and then go away again without saying anything to me. I was very surprised and slightly perturbed by this attention; I could not understand why they were doing this. It seemed to me that I was being taken care of for some purpose, and that they wanted to do something to me later on. I remember that I was always trying to get further away, looking for a hiding-place in case of need. Once I found myself on the main staircase. It was wide, made of marble and covered with a carpet decorated with flowers and beautiful vases. Two tall men, brightly dressed, wearing gloves and very white cravats, sat in silence on each landing. I looked at them in amazement and failed to grasp why they sat there silently, doing nothing except staring at each other.

I came to enjoy these solitary wanderings more and more. Besides, there was another reason for wishing to avoid the upstairs rooms. The Prince's old aunt lived on the upper floor, hardly ever leaving it. This old lady left a sharp impression on my memory. She was unquestionably the most important person in the house. Everyone followed a ceremonious etiquette with her – even the Princess, so proud and self-assured, was obliged on two fixed days of the week to go upstairs and make a personal visit. She usually went in the morning, and a dry conversation would ensue, frequently interrupted by imperious silences as the old lady murmured prayers or counted her beads. The visit was over only when the aunt rose from her chair and kissed the Princess on the lips, thereby indicating that the interview was at an end. Formerly, the Princess had been required to visit her husband's aunt every day, but of late, at the old lady's wish, the severity of her rule had been relaxed and on the five remaining days the Princess was now obliged only to inquire about her health. In general the old lady lived almost like a hermit. She was unmarried and had retired to a convent when she was thirty-five, where she had spent seventeen years without taking the veil; then she had left the convent and moved to Moscow to live with her widowed sister, Countess L., whose health had been deteriorating for years. There she was reconciled with a second sister, the unmarried Princess X., with whom she had been on bad terms for more than twenty years.

But the old ladies are said never to have passed a day without quarrelling; thousands of times they were on the point of parting, but could never do so because they realized that in the end they needed each other as a safeguard against boredom and the infirmities of old age. But in spite of their rather unattractive way of life and the ceremonial boredom that reigned in their Moscow tower chamber, the whole town saw it as a duty to continue visiting the three recluses. They were regarded as the custodians of all the sanctities and traditions of the aristocracy and as the living relics of the original nobility. Countess L. was a wonderful woman who left many pleasant memories behind. People made a point of visiting them first on arrival from Petersburg; once received in their house, they would be received anywhere. But the Countess died, and the sisters parted: the elder Princess remained in Moscow to inherit her share of the fortune of the Countess, who had died childless, while the younger sister, the recluse, settled with her nephew Prince X. in Petersburg. On the other hand, the Prince's two children, Katya and Alexander, were left in Moscow to console and distract their grandmother in her loneliness. The Princess, their mother, who was passionately fond of children, dared not protest at being parted from them for the whole period of mourning. I have omitted to mention that the Prince's entire household was still in mourning when I came to live there, although this soon came to an end.

The old Princess always dressed in black, in gowns of plain woollen material, and she wore starched, pleated collars, which made her look as if she came from the poorhouse. She was never without her rosary, attended Mass formally, observed all the fasts, received visits from ecclesiastical dignitaries and pious persons, read holy books and, all in all, lived like a nun. The silence upstairs was awesome; it was impossible for a door to creak without the Princess, as sharp as a fifteen-year-old, sending instantly to find out the cause, though it might well have been no more than a squeak. Everyone spoke in a whisper and went about on tiptoe; the poor Frenchwoman, an old lady herself, was finally forced to give up her favourite footwear – high-heeled shoes. Heels were banished. A fortnight after my arrival, the old Princess sent to inquire who I was, what I was like, how I came to the house and so on. Her inquiries were swiftly and dutifully answered. Then a second messenger was sent to the Frenchwoman, asking why the Princess had not yet seen me. This instantly caused a commotion; they started combing my hair, washing my hands and my face (which were already very clean) and showing me how to enter, how to bow, how to look more cheerful and gracious, how to speak – in short, I was thoroughly pestered. Then a messenger was sent from our part of the house with the proposal that the great lady might like to see the little orphan. A reply came back in the negative, but a time was appointed for the following day, after Mass. I did not sleep all night, and was told afterwards that I was raving throughout the night about going to visit the old Princess and begging her forgiveness for something. Finally, the hour of my presentation arrived. As I entered the room I saw a withered little old lady sitting in an enormous armchair. She nodded to me and put on her spectacles in order to examine me more closely. I remember that she did not like me at all. She commented on my being almost a savage, ignorant of the proper way to curtsy or kiss a hand. Questions followed, but I was scarcely able to answer and, when she began talking about my father and mother, I burst into tears. The old lady was very displeased at my display of emotion; nevertheless she started to comfort me and advised me to put my trust in God. Then she asked me when I had last been to church and, realizing that I hardly understood the question, for my education had been sorely neglected, she was horrified. She sent for the younger Princess. In the ensuing discussion it was agreed that I should be taken to church the following Sunday. Until then, the Princess promised to pray for me, but she told them to take me away for, in her own words, I had made a very poor impression. There was nothing strange in that; it could hardly have been otherwise. It was evident that she did not like me at all, and the very same day she sent a message to say that I was too noisy and could be heard running about all over the house. As I had spent all day without moving, this was evidently the old lady's fancy. Yet the same message arrived the next day. It happened that I had broken a cup just at that moment. The French governess and all the servants were in despair, and I was immediately sent to a remote room, to which they all followed me in a state of deep panic.

I do not remember how the incident ended, but it was for this reason that I was glad to slip away downstairs, to be alone as I wandered through the spacious rooms, knowing that at least I was not disturbing anyone there.

I remember sitting downstairs in the hallway one day, with my head bowed and my face buried in my hands, remaining like that for hours. I kept on thinking, but my immature mind could not resolve all my misery and grew increasingly forlorn and sorrowful. Suddenly a soft voice spoke over my head: 'What's the matter, my poor child?'

I raised my head; it was the Prince. His face expressed deep sympathy and compassion. I gazed up at him with such a crushed, such an unhappy look that tears welled up in his deep blue eyes.

'Poor little orphan!' he said, patting me on the head.

'No, no, not an orphan, no!' I said, my moans breaking forth and everything inside me surging and churning around. I got up from my seat, clutched his hand, kissing it and drenching it with my tears, and repeated in an imploring tone: 'No, no, not an orphan, no!'

'My child! What's wrong with you, my poor dear Netochka?'

'Where's my mother, where's my mother?' I cried, sobbing loudly, unable to hide my misery any longer, and I fell helplessly on my knees beside him. 'Where's my mother, my darling mother – where is she?'

'Forgive me, my child! ... Oh, poor little thing, I have reminded her ... What have I done! Come, come along with me, Netochka, come along with me.' He took me by the hand and led me swiftly away from the hallway. He was profoundly moved. At length we came to a room I had never seen before.

It was the icon room. It was dusk, and the lamps shone brightly, their lights reflected on the golden rizas and precious stones of the icons. The faces of the saints looked out dimly from their glistening settings. Everything here was so different from any of the other rooms, so mysterious and gloomy, that I was impressed and awed, and my heart was filled with dread. The Prince quickly made me kneel down before the icon of Our Lady. He knelt down beside me . . .

'Pray, my child, pray. We shall both pray,' he said in a soft, broken voice. But I could not pray; I was overwhelmed, even frightened. I recalled my father's words that last night, beside my mother's body, and I had a nervous fit. I lay ill in bed and in this, the second period of my illness, I almost died. This is how it all happened.

One morning a familiar name sounded in my ears. I heard S.'s name pronounced by one of the members of the household who was standing beside my bed. I shuddered; memories surged up and, overwhelmed by recollections, dreams and torments, I lay delirious for goodness knows how many hours, fretting. When I woke up late at night it was dark in the room, the candle had gone out and the maid who usually sat in my room was not there. Then I heard the sound of music in the distance. At times the sound died down entirely; then it grew louder, as if it was coming closer. I do not remember what feeling came over me, or what resolve suddenly arose in my sick brain, but I got out of bed. I do not know where I found the strength, but I dressed in mourning clothes and went groping around the room. There was no one in the next room, nor in the room beyond. At last I made my way into the corridor. The sounds were becoming more and more distinct. In the middle of the corridor was a staircase that I always used when going to the large rooms downstairs. The staircase was brightly illuminated, and people were walking about down below. I hid in a corner until it was possible to pass unnoticed to the second floor. The music was coming from the drawing-room, and I could hear a lot of noisy voices talking, It sounded as if thousands of people were assembled. One of the drawing-room doors, leading into the corridor, was draped with two curtains made of crimson velvet. I lifted one of them and stood between the two. My heart was beating so strongly I could hardly stand upright. However, a few minutes later, having mastered my agitation, I managed to draw back the edge of the second curtain ... My goodness! That large gloomy room which I was so afraid of entering was now ablaze with thousands of candles. It was like a sea of light flooding upon me, and my eyes, accustomed to the darkness, were blinded by its brilliance. The perfumed air was blowing in my face like a warm wind. Millions of people were walking to and fro, and they all seemed to have happy, joyful faces. The women wore expensive, pretty dresses, and wherever I looked I saw eyes sparkling with pleasure. I stood there spellbound. It seemed as if I had seen all this somewhere before, in a dream ... I was reminded of our attic room at dusk, the high window, the street far away below with the glittering lamp-posts, the windows of the house standing opposite with the red curtains, the carriages crowding round the front door, the stamping and snorting of high-spirited horses, the shouts, the noise, the shadows flitting across the windows and the faint, distant music ... So here it was, here was that paradise! The thought flashed through my mind. This is where I had wanted to go with my poor father ... It was not a dream after all! ... Yes, I had seen it all before in my dreams, in my fancies! My imagination, inflamed by illness, caught fire, and I shed tears of ecstasy. I searched for my father. I was sure he was there, and my heart throbbed in anticipation ... I could scarcely breathe ... The music died down, there was a hum of voices, and then a murmur arose from all corners of the room. I gazed anxiously into the faces flashing past, trying to recognize someone. All at once there was an atmosphere of extraordinary excitement in the room. I caught sight of an old man, tall and lean, standing on a raised platform. His pale face smiled as he bent his crooked body, bowing in all directions; in his hands he was holding a violin. A profound silence followed, spreading across the room as if they were all holding their breath. All eyes were fixed expectantly on the old man. He raised his violin and touched the strings with his bow. The music began, and all at once I felt something stab my heart. With infinite yearning, my breath bated, I listened; a familiar sound came to my ears. I seemed to have heard these chords before; it was a kind of foreboding ... a foreboding of something horrible and frightening was reflected in my heart. The music grew louder, swifter, the sound more vital. It was like a wail of despair, a lament, a prayer uttered in vain, echoing through the crowd and dying down in sorrow. An increasingly familiar voice was speaking inside me, but my heart refused to believe it. I clenched my teeth to hold back a groan of pain and grabbed hold of the curtain to prevent myself falling. Occasionally I closed my eyes, and then quickly opened them to peer eagerly at the crowd, imagining that it was a dream and that I would wake up at some terrible, already familiar moment; a dream of that last night, listening to the same music. Opening my eyes, I tried to reassure myself; I looked anxiously into the crowd . . . no – these were different people, different faces. It seemed as if they were all, like me, expecting something, and that we were all suffering together; that they too wanted to scream at the ghastly moans and wails that were tormenting their souls. But the wails and the moans flowed on, more anguished, more plaintive, more prolonged. Then the last, fearful, extended cry rang out, and my inside was wrenched apart . . . There was no longer any doubt: it was the same, the same cry; I recognized it, I had heard it before and, as on the other occasion, it pierced my heart.

'Father, father,' the thought went through my mind in a flash, 'here he is, it's him, he's calling me. It's his violin!'

A groan broke from the crowd and a roar of applause shook the room. I could restrain myself no longer and, throwing back the curtains, I dashed into the room. 'Papa, Papa, it's you! Where are you?' I cried, quite beside myself. I do not know how I reached the tall old man; they let me pass, standing aside to make way for me. I flung myself at him with an anguished shriek; I thought I was embracing my father . . . Suddenly I saw the long bony hands that had seized me, lifting me into the air. Black eyes were fixed on me, as if they wished to consume me with their fire. I looked at the old man. 'No, this isn't father, it's his murderer,' flashed through my mind. A sort of frenzy came over me, and it suddenly seemed that laughter was ringing out above me, reverberating through the room, in one concentrated roar. I lost consciousness.

CHAPTER FIVE

That was the second and the last period of my illness. When I opened my eyes again, I saw a child's face bending over me; it was a girl of my own age, and my first gesture was to hold out my hand to her. From the moment I saw her, a feeling of happiness like a sweet premonition filled my soul. Try to imagine a face of idyllic charm and stunning, dazzling beauty; one of those before which you stop, transfixed in sweet confusion, trembling with delight; a face that makes you grateful for its existence, for allowing your eyes to fall upon it, for passing you by. It belonged to the Prince's daughter, Katya, who had just returned from Moscow. She smiled at my gesture, and my frail nerves ached with a sweet ecstasy.

The little Princess called to her father, who was standing near by, talking to the doctor.

'Well, thank God, thank God,' said the Prince, taking my hand, his face beaming with genuine pleasure. 'I'm so glad, so glad,' he continued with characteristic rapidity. 'And this is my daughter, Katya. Now you will have a friend. Hurry and get well, Netochka. Naughty girl, what a fright she gave me!'

My recovery followed very quickly. A few days later I was already up and about. Every morning Katya came to my bedside, always smiling, always with laughter on her lips. I awaited her visits with tremendous excitement; I longed to kiss her! But the naughty child never stayed longer than a few minutes, for she could not sit still. To be always on the move, running and skipping and making a commotion about the house, was an absolute necessity to her. The very first time I met her, she announced that she could not come more often because it was so dreadfully boring to sit with me, and that she only came because she felt so sorry for me that she could not help coming, and that she felt sure we would get on better once I was well again. And every morning her first words were: 'Well, are you all right now?'

But I was still pale and thin, and as the smile seemed to appear nervously on my doleful face, the little Princess would frown immediately, shaking her head and stamping her feet in annoyance.

'Didn't I tell you to get better? So? I suppose they don't give you anything to eat?'

'A little,' I replied timidly, for I was already overawed by her.

Above all I wanted her to like me, and was nervous about everything I said or did before her. I became more and more enraptured by her visits. While she was with me I could not take my eyes off her and, after she left, I would continue to gaze, spellbound, at the spot where she had been standing. I started to dream of her and, when I was awake, invented lengthy conversations with her in her absence: I would be her friend, playing all sorts of pranks with her and weeping with her when we were scolded. In short, I dreamt of her as if we were in love. I was desperately anxious to get well and put on weight, as she advised, just as quickly as possible.

Sometimes, when Katya came running to me in the morning, calling out, 'Aren't you well yet? Still as thin as ever?', I would cower as if I were guilty of something. But it was incomprehensible to her that I could not make an overnight recovery, and she began getting distinctly cross about it.

'Well, if you like, I'll bring you some cake today,' she said to me one day. 'If you eat it, you'll soon fatten up.'

'Oh yes, do bring me some,' I said, delighted at the prospect of seeing her again.

When she came to inquire about my health, the little Princess usually sat down in a chair opposite me and right away began scrutinizing me with her black eyes. When she first made my acquaintance, she was constantly examining me from head to foot, with naïve astonishment. But conversation between us flagged; I was intimidated by Katya's presence and by her abrupt turnabouts, although I longed to talk to her.

'Why are you so quiet?' Katya began, after one of our silences.

82

'What does your father do?' I asked her, delighted that I had found a sentence with which to start a conversation.

'Nothing. Papa is fine. Today I drank two cups of coffee instead of one. How many did you have?'

'One.'

Silence again.

'Falstaff tried to bite me today.'

'Is that the dog?'

'Yes, haven't you seen him?'

'Yes, I have.'

'Then why ask?' Since I did not know what to answer the Princess, she once again stared at me in astonishment.

'Well? Do you like me coming to talk to you?'

'Yes I do, very much. Come more often.'

'They told me it would cheer you up if I came to see you, but do hurry and get well. I'm going to bring you some cake today ... Why are you always so quiet?'

'I just am.'

'I suppose you're always thinking?'

'Yes, I think a lot.'

'They tell me that I talk too much and think too little. Is it really so bad to be talkative?'

'No, I like it when you talk.'

'Hmm ... I'll ask Madame Léotard, she knows everything. But what do you think about?'

'I think about you,' I answered, after a pause.

'Does it make you happy?'

'Yes.'

'Then that means you must like me?'

'Yes.'

'Well, I don't like you yet. You're so thin. I'm going to bring you that cake. Well, goodbye, then.' Kissing me as she left, the Princess vanished from the room. But after dinner the cake really did arrive. She ran in, frenzied and giggling with glee because she had brought me something to eat that was forbidden.

'Eat it all ... eat more, eat more, it's my cake. I haven't eaten any of it. Well, goodbye.' And that was all I saw of her.

On another occasion she suddenly flew in to see me at an unusual hour, her black curls in wild disarray, her cheeks aflame and her eyes sparkling, which indicated that she had been running and skipping around for an hour or so.

'Can you play badminton?' she cried. She was breathless, and spoke quickly in her rush to be off again.

'No,' I answered, miserable that I could not say yes.

'What a funny thing you are. Well, hurry and get better, then I'll teach you. I only came to find out. Now I'm going to play with Madame Léotard. Goodbye, they're waiting for me.'

Finally I was able to get up for good, although I was still weak and fragile. My first and foremost thought was that I would no longer be separated from Katya. My attraction to her was irresistible; I could not take my eyes off her, which she found surprising. I walked about, burning with this new feeling, in such a way that she could not help noticing it; at first she thought it exceptionally strange. I remember how once, while we were playing a game, I could not restrain myself from throwing my arms around her neck and kissing her. She freed herself from my embrace, grabbed me by the hand and, frowning, as if I had offended her in some way, asked me: 'What are you doing? Why are you kissing me?'

I felt embarrassed, as though I had done something wrong; I was so startled by her abrupt question that I did not answer. The Princess shrugged her shoulders as a sign of her unresolved perplexity (a gesture which became a habit with her) and, squeezing her puffy lips, sat down in the corner of the sofa and stared at me for a long time, as if turning something over in her mind, trying to solve a new puzzle. This, too, was a habit of hers when she found herself in a difficult spot. For my part, it took me a long time to get accustomed to these sudden, sharp manifestations of character.

At first I blamed myself and thought that there really was a lot about me that was strange. Although this was true, I was, none the less, tormented with doubts: why could I not make friends with Katya right from the start, once and for all? This failure grieved me terribly, and I felt ready to cry at every quick word and doubtful look from her. And my grief mounted not by the day but by the hour, because with Katya everything moved so swiftly. Within a few days I noticed that she had taken a dislike to me, and this was even turning into repugnance. Everything this girl did was done swiftly and sharply, one might even have said impetuously, had there not been a true and noble grace in the brusque manifestations of her naïve, open character. It began by her feeling uncertain of me, and then contemptuous. I believe this stemmed from my complete inability to play any kind of game. The Princess loved to frolic and romp around; she was strong, lively and nimble, while I was the exact opposite. I was still weak from my illness, quiet and thoughtful, and I did not enjoy playing. In fact, I was entirely lacking in all the qualities that appealed to Katya. Apart from this, I could not bear to feel that I was displeasing to anyone. Immediately I began to feel gloomy, and as my spirits sank I lost the strength to smooth over my mistakes or to improve on the poor impression I had made. In short, I was in a hopeless position, and Katya was unable to understand this. At first she even frightened me; she would look at me in astonishment (another of her habits) after having spent an hour or more struggling to teach me how to play badminton without success. And then, as I instantly became depressed and the tears welled up in my eyes, she would ponder for a moment or two and, failing to make sense of me or of her own feelings, she would dash off to play by herself without asking me to join her, possibly not speaking to me again for days. I was taken aback by this behaviour, and could barely endure her disdain. This new loneliness became almost as painful to me as my previous one, and again I started to grow gloomy and pensive. Once more my heart was burdened with dark thoughts.

Madame Léotard, who looked after us, eventually became aware of the change in our relationship. As soon as she noticed my enforced solitude, she went directly to the little Princess and reprimanded her for being unable to get along with me. The Princess frowned, shrugged her shoulders and announced that there was nothing she could do with me; that I did not know how to play, that I was always thinking about something and that she had better wait for her brother, Sasha, who was coming from Moscow, and then she would be much happier.

Madame Léotard was not satisfied with this answer and reminded Katya that she was leaving me on my own when I was still unwell and that I could not be as cheerful and playful as she herself, which was, incidentally, no bad thing, since she was too lively. She went on to remind her that three days ago she had almost been bitten by the bulldog, and she thoroughly scolded her. She ended by sending Katya to me, bidding her make it up with me at once.

Katya listened to Madame Léotard very attentively, as if she had actually detected something new and reasonable in her reproaches. Deserting her hoop, which she had been rolling around the hall, she came up to me with a very serious air, saying: 'Would you like to play?'

'No,' I answered, afraid both for myself and for Katya after Madame Léotard's scolding.

'Then what would you like to do?'

'I'll just sit here. I get tired running around, but don't be cross with me, Katya, because I do like you very much.'

'All right then, I'll play by myself,' said Katya, quietly and deliberately, as if surprised to find that she was, as it turned out, not to blame.

'Goodbye then, and I'm not cross with you.'

'Goodbye,' I answered, getting up and offering her my hand.

'Perhaps you'd like me to kiss you?' she asked, after thinking a little. Probably she recalled our recent scene and was trying to be as nice as possible to me in order to be rid of me as quickly and pleasantly as she could.

'As you like,' I answered, with a faint hope. She came up to me and, very seriously, without smiling, kissed me. Having thus fulfilled her obligations, having done even more than was asked of her to make it up with the poor little girl to whom she had been sent, she ran off, satisfied and cheerful. Before long, her laughter and shouting was heard echoing through the house until, exhausted and completely out of breath, she threw herself down on to the sofa to rest and gather new strength. All that evening she kept looking at me suspiciously; she probably thought I was a very strange individual. I could tell that she wanted to discuss something with me, to clear up some doubt about me that was on her mind, but on that occasion – why, I do not know – she restrained herself.

Katya usually had her lessons in the morning. Madame Léotard was teaching her French; her instruction consisted of going over the grammar and reading selections from La Fontaine. Katya was not given much in the way of lessons, because it was enough of a job to persuade her to sit still with her books for two hours a day. She had reluctantly agreed to this arrangement at her father's request and her mother's insistence, and followed it through conscientiously because she had given her word. She had the rare gift of being able to grasp things quickly and easily. But even here she had her little idiosyncrasies: if she did not understand something, she immediately started working it out for herself, because she found it humiliating to have something explained to her. Apparently there were times when she spent whole days struggling over a problem which she was unable to solve, and she became angry if she could not find the answer without someone else's help. Only as a last resort, when she was completely exhausted, would she turn to Madame Léotard for help with a question that had baffled her. It was the same with everything she did. Although it was not immediately obvious, she did think a great deal. At the same time, she was naïve for her age. Sometimes she would ask questions which were utterly silly, while at other times her responses revealed a most penetrating subtlety and intelligence.

At length, when I was well enough to study a bit, Madame Léotard examined me to see how much I knew. When she discovered that I could read well but that my writing was poor, she decided that she had to start teaching me French at once. I had no objections, and one morning I found myself sitting at the school table with Katya. As it turned out, Katya was very dull and scatterbrained that day, so much so that Madame Léotard was at a loss what to do. In an effort to please my teacher, I, on the other hand, managed to master the whole of the French alphabet in one sitting. By the end of the lesson Madame Léotard was distinctly angry with Katya.

'Look at her,' she said, pointing to me, 'a sick child, and yet in her first lesson she's done ten times more than you. Aren't you ashamed?' Katya thought for a moment, and then her face flushed as red as a beetroot, proving the accuracy of Madame Léotard's reproach. Katya's first reaction to any kind of failure, disappointment, indignation, or shame at being caught doing something naughty – to anything, in fact – was to turn red and burn with shame. On this occasion she forced back her tears and, saying nothing, she merely looked at me as if she wanted to chew me up. I quickly guessed what was wrong. The poor girl was proud and thoroughly egocentric. When we left Madame Léotard, I wanted to dispel her vexation as quickly as possible by convincing her that I was not to blame for what the governess had said to her. But Katya remained silent, as if she did not hear me.

An hour later she came into the room where I was sitting over a book, still thinking about her, stunned and dismayed that once again she would not speak to me. Glancing at me mistrustfully, she sat down as usual on the sofa and gazed firmly at me for the next half-hour. Finally, unable to bear this any longer, I gave her an inquiring glance.

'Do you know how to dance?' asked Katya.

'No, I don't.'

'Well I do.'

Silence.

'Can you play the piano?'

'No, I can't do that either.'

'I can. It's very difficult.'

I made no response.

'Madame Léotard said that you're cleverer than me.'

'Madame Léotard was cross with you,' I answered.

'Do you think Papa will be cross too?'

'I don't know,' I replied.

Silence again. The Princess tapped her little foot on the floor impatiently.

'And are you going to make fun of me now, just because you're cleverer than I am?' she said at last, recognizing her chagrin.

'Oh no, no!' I cried, jumping up and throwing my arms around her. Suddenly we heard Madame Léotard's voice. She had been observing and listening to our conversation for the last five minutes.

'Aren't you ashamed of thinking such a thing, let alone asking it? Shame on you, Princess!' she continued. 'You've become jealous of the poor child and so you start boasting about dancing and playing the piano. Disgraceful! I shall tell the Prince everything.' The Princess's cheeks glowed like a sunset. 'What a nasty thing to do. You've offended her with your questions. Her parents were poor and could not hire teachers for her. She studied by herself, because she's got a good honest heart. You should love her, rather than always wishing to quarrel. Shame on you! Shame on you! She's an orphan; she has no one. Next you'll start boasting that you're a Princess and she isn't. I'll leave you alone now, to think about what I've just said and mend your ways.'

The Princess thought about it for two days! For two days her laughter and cries were not to be heard. Waking in the night, I could hear her arguing with Madame Léotard even in her sleep. She even grew a little thinner during those two days; her normally rosy cheeks were not as colourful as usual. At last, on the third day, we happened to meet each other in the large rooms downstairs. The Princess was leaving her mother's apartment, but when she saw me she sat down near by, facing me. I waited in nervous anticipation of what might happen. I was trembling all over.

'Netochka, why did I have to be scolded on account of you?' she finally asked.

'It was not on account of me, Katya,' I hastened to correct her.

'But Madame Léotard says that I offended you.'

'No, Katya dear, no, you didn't offend me.'

The Princess shrugged her shoulders, perplexed.

'Then why are you always crying?' she asked after a brief silence.

'I won't cry, if that's what you want,' I answered through my tears.

She shrugged her shoulders again.

'Did you always cry a lot?'

I did not answer.

'Why have you come to live with us?' the Princess asked abruptly, after another short pause.

I felt as if my heart was being pierced, and I looked at her in dismay.

'Because I'm an orphan,' I answered finally, mustering my courage.

'Did you have a Mama and Papa?'

'Yes, I did!'

'Didn't they love you?'

'Yes, they did,' I said. I needed all the strength I had.

'Were they poor?'

'Yes.'

'Didn't they teach you anything?'

'They taught me to read.'

'Did you have any toys?'

'No.'

'Did you eat cake?'

'No.'

'How many rooms did you have?'

'One.'

'One room?'

'One.'

'What about the servants?'

'There were no servants.'

'Then who did the work?'

'I did the shopping.'

The Princess's questions became increasingly painful. All the memories, my loneliness, and the Princess's incredulity struck a cruel note in my already bleeding heart. I was shaking with emotion and choking back tears.

'You must be pleased to be living with us?'

I was silent.

'Did you have pretty dresses?'

'No.'

'Did you have ugly ones?'

'Yes.'

'I saw your dress, they showed it to me.'

'Why are you asking me these things?' I said, jumping up from my chair and trembling with this new, unbelievable sensation. 'Why are you asking me these things?' I repeated, blushing in indignation. 'Why are you making fun of me?' The Princess flared up and also jumped up from her chair, but swiftly gained control of herself.

'I'm not making fun of you,' she said. 'I only wanted to find out whether it was true that your father and mother were poor.'

'Why are you asking me about my father and mother?' I cried, bursting into tears of heartfelt anguish. 'Why are you asking me about them in this way? What have they ever done to you, Katya?' Katya was bewildered and did not know what to say. At that moment the Prince came in.

'What's the matter, Netochka?' he asked, seeing me in tears. 'What's the matter?' he repeated, after glancing at Katya, whose face was bright red. 'What have you been talking about? Have you been quarrelling? ... Netochka, what are you two quarrelling about?' Unable to give an answer, I grasped the Prince's hand and kissed it, covering it in tears.

'Katya, don't lie! What's been happening here?'

But Katya was incapable of lying.

'I told her I had seen what an ugly dress she wore when she lived with her father and mother.'

'Who showed it to you? Who dared?'

'I saw it myself,' said Katya resolutely.

'Very well then! I know you well enough, and I trust that you won't tell tales. And what else?'

'She started to cry and asked me why I was making fun of her father and mother.'

'Then you were making fun of them?'

Although she had not actually been making fun of them it had been her intention: this I had realized from the beginning. She gave no response, implying that she admitted to the offence.

'Ask her forgiveness immediately,' said the Prince, pointing to me. The Princess, who was as white as a sheet, did not move.

'Well?' said the Prince.

'I don't want to, I don't want to!' she suddenly shouted, flashing her eyes and stamping her feet. 'I don't want to ask her forgiveness, Papa. I don't like her and I don't want to live with her any longer. It's not my fault that she spends all day crying. I don't want to, I don't want to.'

'Come with me,' said the Prince, taking her by the hand and leading her into his study. 'Netochka, go upstairs.' I wanted to rush over to him, I wanted to plead for Katya, but the Prince sternly repeated his order and I went upstairs, frozen and half-dead with fear. When I reached our room I collapsed on to the sofa and buried my head in my hands. I counted the minutes as I waited impatiently for Katya to return; I wanted to throw myself at her feet. When she did finally come, she walked straight past me and sat down in a corner. Her eyes were red and her cheeks were puffy from crying. All my resolve disappeared. I watched her in fear; I was too afraid to move.

I did my utmost to blame myself and genuinely tried to persuade myself that it was all my fault. A thousand times I wanted to go to Katya, and a thousand times I hesitated, not knowing how she would react to me. Thus the second day passed. But on the third day, towards evening, Katya cheered up and started bowling her hoop around the room. This did not, however, last long, and she soon returned to her corner. Just before bedtime she suddenly turned towards me, took a step in my direction, and opened her mouth to say something – but she stopped short, turned round and went to bed. Another day went by in this fashion, and Madame Léotard began to grow concerned about Katya. She asked her why she was so white, and whether she was ill. Katya did not answer. She looked around for her shuttlecock, but as soon as she had turned away from Madame Léotard she blushed and began to cry. She ran out of the room so that I would not see her tears. In the end it all died down. Exactly three days after our argument, she suddenly appeared in the room and, approaching me with a certain diffidence, said: 'Papa says I must ask your forgiveness. Do you forgive me?' Breathless with excitement, I threw my arms around her.

'Yes, yes, I do,' I said.

'Papa says I must kiss you. Will you give me a kiss?' In reply, I started kissing her hands, smothering them in tears. When I looked at Katya I saw something I had never seen before. Her lips and her chin were quivering, and her eyes were moist; but in a short time she had overcome her agitation and, in a flash, a smile broke out on her lips.

'I'll go and tell Papa that I've kissed you and asked for your forgiveness,' she said softly, as if she was reflecting. 'I haven't seen him for three days; he forbade me to go near his room until I'd done this,' she added, after a pause. After saying this she went downstairs, timidly and thoughtfully, as if unsure of how her father would receive her.

An hour later, the noise of laughter and shouting, followed by Falstaff's barks, resounded from upstairs; then the clatter of something falling over and breaking, and books flying to the floor. When I once again heard the sound of her hoop spinning across the room, I knew that Katya had made things up with her father, and my heart began throbbing with joy.

But she did not come near me and was evidently avoiding having to talk to me. Instead I was in the special position of having aroused her curiosity. She sat down opposite me where she could inspect me more closely and stared with increasing intensity. Her look became more naïve than ever. In short, this spoilt, wilful girl, who was fussed over and mollycoddled by everyone in the house, could not understand how I had more than once crossed her path when she had absolutely no wish to find me there. But she had a sweet and generous little heart, which always led her in the right direction, if only through instinct. The greatest influence over her was her father, whom she adored. Her mother loved her to distraction, but was terribly strict with her. It was from her that Katya had inherited her wilfulness, her pride and her powerful character. But her mother had whims which amounted to a kind of moral tyranny. The Princess had a rather peculiar notion of raising a child, and Katya's upbringing was a strange combination of pampering and ruthless severity. What was permitted on one day was, for no given reason, forbidden the next. This outraged Katya's concept of justice . . . But that story comes later. Let me just mention that she was already capable of distinguishing between her relations with her father and with her mother. With the former she was herself – open, frank and unarmed – while with her mother she was just the opposite – reticent, mistrustful but unquestioningly obedient. However, her obedience did not spring from conviction or sincerity, but was given merely because it belonged to the prescribed order of things. This I shall explain later. To be fair to Katya, I must say that she understood her mother and, in submitting to her, she was nevertheless fully aware of her boundless love. That this love was at times morbidly excessive was a circumstance of which Katya took full advantage. Alas, it was an advantage that was to prove of small assistance to the hot-headed little girl.

But *I* could barely understand what was happening to me. Everything inside me seemed so disturbed by this new and unfamiliar emotion, and I am not exaggerating if I say that I suffered agonies from it and was torn apart by it. To be brief, and forgive me for what I am now about to say, I was in love with Katya. Yes, it was love, real love with all its ups and downs, real passionate love. What was it that attracted me to her? What had instigated such love? It began when I first set eyes on her, when all my emotions were sweetly aroused by the appearance of such a charming, angelic-looking child. Everything about her was so beautiful; none of her feelings was ingrained, but all had been implanted in her, and came out at moments of conflict. It was apparent to everyone that her original beauty had, with time, acquired a false form; but everything about her, from that conflict forward, glowed with gratifying hope, heralding a splendid future. It was not only I who loved and admired her, but everyone. When we went out for our three o'clock walk, passers-by used to stop in amazement, simply to look at her, and quite often exclamations of delight echoed after this fortunate child. She was born for happiness, she must have been; that was the first impression she gave. Perhaps what had first struck me was an aesthetic appreciation, an exquisite sensation of awakened beauty speaking for the first time, and therein lay the source of my increasing love.

The little Princess's main failing, or rather the aspect of her character which strove irrepressibly for embodiment in a natural form and which clearly found itself in decline when she was in a state of conflict, was her pride. This pride extended itself to innocent trifles and fell into egocentricity. If, for example, she met with any contradiction whatsoever, she was not so much offended or angered as surprised. She could not conceive of anything being other than what she wished it to be. Nevertheless, her sense of justice always conquered her heart's instincts. When she was convinced that she was wrong, she conceded immediately and no more was heard or said. And if her attitude towards me changed during that period, I can best explain it as an incomprehensible antipathy to me that was troubling her equilibrium. It must have been that; she entered into her enthusiasms with too much passion, and she was ultimately led to the correct path by example and experience. The results of all her endeavours were beautiful and sincere, but they were achieved at the cost of continual deviation and error.

Katya very soon satisfied her curiosity about me, and finally she decided to leave me in peace. She behaved as if I was not even living in the house and refused to address a single superfluous word to me. Indeed she hardly even offered the necessary words. I was excluded from all her games, but it was done so cunningly that it almost seemed that I had agreed to it. Our lessons followed their usual course and, if I was held up to her as an example of quick-wittedness and sobriety, I no longer had the honour of wounding her vanity, which was extremely delicate and could even be hurt by the bulldog, Sir John Falstaff. Falstaff was a cold-blooded, phlegmatic animal, but as fierce as a tiger when teased – fierce enough to defy his master. Another trait was that he definitely loved nobody; but his worst natural enemy was unquestionably the old Princess ... However, that story comes later. Vain Katya tried everything possible to overcome Falstaff's hostility. She did not like to think that there could be anyone in the house who did not recognize her authority, her power, and who did not bow to her and love her. And so she resolved to attack Falstaff herself. She wanted to dominate and command everyone, so how could Falstaff refuse to comply? However, the stubborn bulldog refused to give in to her.

One day, after lunch, when we were both sitting downstairs in the large hallway, the bulldog was stretched out in the middle of the room enjoying his afternoon nap. This was the precise moment that Katya took it into her head to conquer him with her will. And so she abandoned her game and crept over to him on tiptoe, beckoning him with coaxing gestures and calling him by fond pet names. But even before she managed to get near him, he bared his terrible fangs, and the Princess stopped. She had intended to go up to him and stroke him (something he permitted no one to do but Katya's mother, to whom he belonged), and afterwards to persuade him to follow her, a difficult and risky task, since Falstaff would have no hesitation in biting her hand and tearing her to pieces if he felt the need. He was as strong as a bear, and I watched Katya's manoeuvres, anxious and alarmed, from a distance. But it was hard to move her once she had decided on something, and the sight of Falstaff's teeth, bared most uncivilly, was insufficient to deter her. When she realized the impossibility of reaching him directly, the Princess found herself in a quandary and began circling her enemy. Falstaff did not stir. Katya made a second attempt, reducing her circle. Then she went round him for the third time but, when she reached the point considered by Falstaff as a sacred territory, he bared his teeth again. The Princess stamped her feet, walked off and sat down, vexed and thoughtful, on the sofa.

Ten minutes later she had devised a new method of seduction and quickly went out, returning with a handful of biscuits and cakes. In other words, she had changed her tactics. But Falstaff remained quite indifferent, probably because he had just eaten his fill. He did not even bother to look at the biscuit which she tossed at him. When the Princess once again approached Falstaff's forbidden boundary, there was opposition, this time stronger than before. Falstaff raised his head, bared his teeth and, with a growl, he began to move. The Princess flushed with anger, threw down the cakes and went back to her seat.

She sat in extreme agitation, beating her feet against the carpet, her cheeks flaming like the sunset and her eyes brimming with tears of annoyance. She happened to look across at me, and it seemed that the blood rushed to her head. She sprang up and, with a distinctly determined step, walked straight up to the fierce dog.

Perhaps astonishment had too powerful an effect on Falstaff this time. He allowed his enemy to cross the boundary, and not until Katya was just a few steps away did he greet the foolish girl with a vicious snarl. Katya stopped short for a moment, and then advanced with determination. I was shivering with fear. I had never seen her so excited; her eyes were flashing with victory and triumph. She would have made a wonderful picture: she stood her ground so boldly before the menacing glare of the infuriated bulldog and did not flinch at the sight of his jaws. He sat up, and a horrible growl came from his hairy belly; another moment and he would have torn her to shreds. But with a majestic gesture the Princess put her little hand on his back and gave him three triumphant strokes. For an instant the dog seemed uncertain. That was the most alarming moment; then all at once he moved. Raising himself laboriously to his feet, stretching himself and probably deciding that it was not worth wasting his time with children, he walked calmly out of the room. The Princess proudly took her position on the conquered territory and looked at me with strange eyes; joyous and giddy with victory. Noticing that I was as white as a sheet, she smiled. But suddenly her cheeks turned deathly white and, hardly able to reach the sofa, she sank down in a near-faint.

My infatuation for Katya already knew no bounds. From that day, when I experienced such great fear on her behalf, I was no longer in control of myself. I pined with love for her, and thousands of times I was on the verge of throwing my arms around her neck, but fear would root me to the spot. I remember that I tried to avoid her so that she would not see my agitation. Once she unexpectedly entered the room where I was hiding. I was very upset, and my heart throbbed so painfully that I felt dizzy. I believed that the little imp noticed this, and for a day or two seemed to be in a state of confusion herself. However, she soon reconciled herself to this state of affairs. A whole month passed, for the course of which I continued to suffer in silence. My feelings were characterized by unbelievable powers of

97

endurance, if one may express it in such a way. My character is notable for its high capacity for suffering, and only in moments of crisis does any sudden manifestation of feeling occur. It should be remembered that throughout this period I had barely exchanged half a dozen words with Katya, but from certain elusive signs I very slowly began to notice that this was not so much due to her forgetfulness or indifference to me as to her deliberate avoidance of me, as if she had promised herself to keep me at a certain distance. For my part, I could no longer sleep at night, and during the day I was unable to conceal my confusion from Madame Léotard. My love for Katya verged on the abnormal. On one occasion I secretly stole one of her handkerchiefs, and on another a piece of ribbon that she used for tying her hair, and I used to kiss them all night long, wiping my tears with them. In the beginning I had been hurt and even mortified by Katya's indifference, but then everything became cloudy and I could not rationalize my feelings. In this way, new impressions gradually crowded out the old ones, and the memories of my gruesome past lost their crippling power and were replaced by a new life.

I remember sometimes waking up in the night, getting out of bed and tiptoeing over to the Princess, and in the dim light of our night lamp standing there for hours, gazing as she slept. Sometimes I sat down on the bed beside her and, bending down, I felt her warm breath on my face. Silently, and trembling with fear, I would kiss her hands, her hair, her shoulders, and her little feet, if they were peeping out of the blankets. Gradually I began to notice, for I had not let her out of my sight for a whole month, that Katya was becoming more thoughtful by the day. She was beginning to lose her even temper: sometimes not a sound was heard from her all day, while at other times she raised an unprecedented racket. She became irritable and demanding; she frequently blushed and lost her temper, and even began performing little acts of cruelty on me. All of a sudden she would refuse to sit next to me at dinner, as if I repelled her; or she would unexpectedly go and see her mother and spend all day with her, knowing well that I was pining in her absence; or she would stare at me for hours, until I did not know what to do with myself for embarrassment, and I would blush and turn pale by turns, never daring to get up and leave the room. On two occasions Katya complained of feeling feverish, although she had never been known to suffer from any kind of illness before. Then, one morning, special arrangements were made. At her express wish, the little Princess was being moved downstairs to the apartments of her mother, whose hair had almost turned white when she heard of Katya's complaint of feeling unwell. It must be pointed out that Katya's mother was exceedingly displeased with me and with the changes she noticed in her daughter, which she ascribed to me and to the influence of what she called my sullen nature. She would have separated us long before, but she had postponed it for the time being, knowing that she would have to endure a serious argument with the Prince, who, though usually yielding to her in everything, could at times be very adamant. She understood the Prince perfectly.

I was stunned by the Princess's move and spent a whole week in a state of heartbroken agitation. I was tormented with grief and racked my brain for the cause of Katya's dislike. My heart was torn with sorrow and indignation, and a sense of injustice rose up in my wounded heart. I developed a sort of pride, and when Katya and I met for our daily walk I looked at her so seriously and independently, so differently from ever before, that she was quite astonished. These changes in me only occurred sporadically, and of course my heart ached more and more afterwards. I grew weaker and feebler than ever. Finally one morning, to my amazement, the little Princess came back upstairs. The first thing she did was to fling herself around Madame Léotard's neck with a shout of wild glee. Then she announced she had returned to us. After nodding at me, she begged to be excused from her lesson that day and proceeded to spend all the morning frolicking and prancing about. I had never before seen her so lively and happy. But towards evening she grew quiet and dreamy, and again a look of sadness clouded her charming little face. When her mother came up to see her in the evening, I could see that Katya was making an unnatural effort to appear cheerful. But as soon as her mother had gone, she broke into tears. I was bewildered. When she saw my concern, the Princess left the room. In short, some sort of unseen crisis was brewing up inside her. Her mother consulted doctors, sent for Madame Léotard every day to question her in minute detail about her daughter, and gave instructions for a constant watch to be kept over her. I alone sensed the truth, and my heart throbbed in hope.

In reality, the little romance was unfolding and drawing to an end. The third day after Katya's return upstairs, she kept looking at me all morning with a lovely sparkle in her eyes and with a long, penetrating gaze . . . Several times I met her look, and each time we both blushed and lowered our eyes, as if ashamed. At last the Princess broke into a laugh and walked off. The clock struck three, and we had to dress ourselves for our walk. Katya suddenly came up to me.

'Your shoelace is undone,' she said. 'Let me tie it for you.' I started bending down to tie it myself, blushing red as a cherry because Katya had at last spoken to me.

'Let me do it!' she said impatiently, and laughed. She bent down and, taking hold of my foot firmly, she placed it on her knee and tied my shoe. I sighed deeply; I was beside myself with a sort of sweet terror. When the shoe was tied she stood up, examining me from head to foot.

'Your throat is not covered,' she said, gently touching my bare neck with her little finger. 'There! Let me wrap it up.' I made no objection as she untied my kerchief and tied it again in her own way. 'Otherwise you may get a cough,' she said with a mischievous smile, her misty black eyes twinkling at me.

I was quite beside myself. I knew neither what was happening to me nor what had come over Katya. But, thank God, our walk was soon over. If it had lasted much longer I doubt whether I could have refrained from rushing over to kiss her in the street. However, as we went upstairs, I managed to give her a stealthy kiss on the shoulder. She noticed, quivered but did not say a word. In the evening she was dressed up and taken downstairs to the Princess, who had visitors. But that night there was a terrible commotion in the house.

Katya was struck by one of her attacks of nerves, and her mother was beside herself with fright. The doctor came and did not know what to say. Everything was put down to children's illnesses and, of course, to Katya's age – but I thought otherwise. In the morning she appeared again upstairs looking rosy, cheerful and incredibly healthy, but she was full of whims and fancies that were not very typical of her.

In the first place, she refused to listen to Madame Léotard throughout the morning. Then she suddenly took it into her head to go and see the old Princess. Contrary to her usual practice, the old lady – who loathed her grand-niece, was always at odds with her, and never wished to see her – on this occasion consented to her visit. It started off all right, and they managed to get along harmoniously for an hour. First of all, the little rascal had decided to beg forgiveness for all her misdemeanours, for her noisy play, and for shouting and disturbing her aunt. With tears in her eyes, the old Princess solemnly forgave her. But then the imp went too far. She took it into her head to tell her aunt about pranks which were as yet no more than schemes and projects for the future, and then meekly and piously pretended to have repented of them. The narrow-minded old lady was most delighted. Her vanity was flattered by the prospect of victory over Katya, the pet and idol of the entire household, who was even capable of making her mother succumb to her whims. And thus the little Princess admitted that first she had intended to pin a visiting card to the Princess's dress; then to hide Falstaff under the bed; then to break her spectacles; then to remove all her books and replace them with her mother's French novels; then to scatter bits of wool all over the floor; then to hide a pack of cards in the old lady's pocket, and so on. In short, each prank grew worse than the last. The old lady was at last beside herself, and her face went from red to white with rage. At last Katya could keep it up no longer, burst into giggles and ran away from her. The Princess lost no time in sending for Katya's mother. There was a fearful to-do, and the mother spent a couple of hours pleading tearfully with her aunt to forgive Katya on account of her being ill. At first the old lady refused to listen to her; she declared that she was leaving the house the next day, and only relented when Katya's mother promised she would postpone her punishment until her daughter was recovered, but that she would then satisfy the old lady's indignation. Katya, however, was severely reprimanded and taken downstairs to her mother.

But, after dinner, the rascal shot off. Creeping downstairs, I met her on the staircase. She had opened the door and was calling Falstaff. Instantly I suspected her of plotting some kind of terrible revenge, which was precisely what she was doing. The old Princess had no more irreconcilable enemy than Falstaff. He was not friendly to anyone; he loved nobody and was aloof, proud and extremely conceited. Although he loved no one, he demanded respectful treatment from everyone, and all were aware of this, while at the same time feeling justifiably frightened by him. But with the sudden arrival of the old Princess in the house, everything had changed. Falstaff was dreadfully insulted, for he was absolutely forbidden to go upstairs. This made him frantic with resentment, and for a whole week he continually scratched at the door at the foot of the stairs leading to the little room above. However, he soon guessed the reason for his banishment and, on the first Sunday, as soon as his mistress had gone to church, Falstaff made for the old lady, barking and yelping. It was with difficulty that they rescued her from the cruel vengeance of the offended dog. From that day onwards Falstaff was strictly forbidden to go upstairs, and whenever the Princess came down he was banished to a remote room. The servants were held strictly responsible for seeing to this. But the avenging creature had managed to break into the upstairs rooms on three occasions. As soon as he reached the top of the stairs, he tore through the whole suite of rooms, making straight for the old Princess's bedroom. Nothing could stop him. Fortunately her door was always kept shut, so all Falstaff could do was to howl madly in front of it, which he would do until the servants ran up and chased him downstairs. During these visits from the fearsome dog, the old Princess screamed as if she were being devoured by him, and on each occasion the fright made her ill. Several times she presented her niece with an ultimatum, and once she went so far as to declare that either Falstaff or she must leave the house. But Katya's mother refused to part with the dog.

The Princess was not fond of many people and, after her children, Falstaff was dearer to her than anyone in the world, and with reason. One day, six years earlier, the Prince had returned from a walk bringing with him a sick, dirty, sorrowful-looking little puppy, though he was a bulldog of excellent pedigree. The Prince had in some way saved the dog's life. The newcomer had behaved in such a gross and unseemly manner that the Princess insisted on his being consigned to the back-yard, where he was kept tied to the end of a rope. The Prince did not object. Two years later, while the family was at the Prince's summer villa, little Sasha, Katya's younger brother, fell into the river Neva. The Princess screamed, and her first thought was to throw herself into the water after her son. She was only held back from the risk of death with great difficulty. In the meantime her son was being rapidly carried away by a strong current, with only his clothes still visible on the surface of the water. They quickly untied the boat, but his rescue would have been a miracle. Suddenly an enormous bulldog plunged into the water just in front of the drowning child, grabbed him with his teeth and swam triumphantly with him to the bank. The Princess threw her arms around the wet, muddy dog and kissed him. Falstaff, who at that time bore the prosaic and very ordinary name of Friska, hated being kissed by anyone, and responded to the Princess's kisses and embraces by biting her shoulder. The Princess suffered from the wound for the rest of her life, but her gratitude was boundless. Falstaff was brought to live inside the house, brushed, washed and adorned with an intricately carved silver collar. He was enthroned on a magnificent bearskin rug in the Princess's sitting-room, and before long she was able to stroke him without being frightened of instant retaliation. She had been horrified to learn that her pet had been called Friska and immediately began the quest for another name, one that was as old as possible. But names like Hector and Cerebus were already too commonplace, and a name more appropriate to the household pet was needed. In the end, the Prince, with Friska's phenomenal voracity in mind, suggested calling him Falstaff. The suggestion was eagerly accepted, and this became the bull-dog's name. Falstaff behaved very well. Like a true Englishman, he was taciturn and morose, and never attacked anyone un-provoked; he only insisted that everyone should respect his bearskin rug as sacred and that he was treated with equal courtesy.

Occasionally, Falstaff was apparently overcome by an attack of spleen as he remembered that his enemy, his irreconcilable enemy who had encroached on his rights, remained un-punished. Thus Falstaff made his way stealthily to the foot of stairs that led to the upper floor. Finding the door closed as usual, he lay down somewhere near by, hiding in a corner and craftily waiting for someone inadvertently to leave the door open. At times the vengeful animal could lie in wait as long as three days, but strict orders had been given to watch the door, and it had been three months since he had last managed to get upstairs.

'Falstaff, Falstaff!' called Katya, as she opened the door and started to beckon and coax him to us, over on the stairs. This time Falstaff, sensing that the door was about to be opened, prepared to leap across his Rubicon. But it was improbable to him that Katya's calls could be real, and he refused to believe his ears. He was as wily as a fox and, so as not to reveal that he had noticed the careless opening of the door, he went over to the window, put his mighty paws on the windowsill and gazed out at the building opposite. In short, he behaved as dis-interestedly as a man who has gone out for a walk and stops for a minute to admire the architecture of a neighbouring build-ing. Meanwhile his heart throbbed as he waited in sweet expectation. And what astonishment and frantic joy when not only was the door opened wide before him, but he was beckoned, invited, implored to go upstairs and wreak his ven-geance without delay! Yelping with delight and baring his teeth, he shot fiercely and triumphantly up the stairs like an arrow. His impetus was so great that a chair which happened to be in the way was overturned and catapulted seven feet away. Falstaff flew like a cannonball. Madame Léotard screamed in horror, but by then he had already reached the forbidden door and, scratching it ferociously with his front paws, was howling like a lost soul. In response came a fearful shriek from the old maid inside. A whole legion of his enemies was flocking from all quarters; the entire household was moving upstairs, and Falstaff, the terrible Falstaff, with a muzzle clapped deftly over his jaw and his four paws tied in a noose, was ignominiously withdrawn from the field of battle and dragged downstairs on the end of a rope.

An envoy was sent to the old Princess.

On this occasion Katya's mother was not so ready to forgive and show mercy – but whom could she punish? She guessed at once, and her glance fell on Katya. So, it was her! Katya stood pale and trembling with fear. Not until then had the poor thing thought about the consequences of her prank. Suspicion might have fallen on one of the servants or an innocent person; but Katya was prepared to tell the whole truth.

'Are you responsible?' the Princess asked sternly.

Seeing Katya's deathly pallor, I stepped forward and firmly declared: 'I let Falstaff go up ... by accident,' I added, my courage suddenly disappearing before the Princess's ominous gaze.

'Madame Léotard! See that she is properly punished!' said the Princess, and she left the room. I glanced at Katya. She stood there stunned, her arms hanging limply at her side and her pale little face looking down at the floor.

The only punishment administered to the Prince's children was to shut them up in an empty room. It was nothing to sit in an empty room for a couple of hours. But when a child is forcibly confined there, against her will, and told that she is deprived of her freedom, the punishment is considerable. Normally Katya and her brother were shut up for two hours. In view of the gravity of my offence, I was shut up for four. I went into my dungeon dizzy with joy. I thought about the little Princess. I knew that I had scored a victory. But instead of four hours later, it was four o'clock in the morning before I was freed. This is what happened.

Two hours after my imprisonment, Madame Léotard learnt that her daughter had arrived from Moscow, but had suddenly fallen ill and wished to see her. Madame Léotard went at once, forgetting all about me. The maid who looked after us probably thought I had been released. Katya had been sent for by her mother and was obliged to sit with her until eleven o'clock. When she returned upstairs, she was extremely surprised to discover that I was not in bed. The maid undressed her and put her to bed, but the Princess had her own reasons for not asking after me. She lay down and waited for me, knowing that my confinement should last for four hours and presuming that Nastya, our nanny, would bring me back. But Nastya had also forgotten about me, chiefly because I always undressed myself. Thus I was left to spend the night in prison.

At four o'clock in the night I heard someone knocking at the door and trying to force it open. I was asleep, having somehow curled up on the floor. I cried out in alarm as I was woken. But I instantly recognized Katya's voice ringing out above the rest; then the voices of Madame Léotard, the terrified Nastya and the housekeeper. At last the door opened and, with tears in her eyes, Madame Léotard took me in her arms and begged me to forgive her for having forgotten me. I flung myself around her neck, weeping. I was shivering with cold and my bones ached from lying on the bare floor. I searched for Katya, but she had run back to our bedroom and leapt into bed; when I returned she was already asleep, or pretending to be. She had been waiting for me all night, but had involuntarily fallen asleep and woken up at four. She raised a commotion, a real uproar, waking up Madame Léotard, who had returned, the nanny, and all the servants. She then obtained my release. By morning the whole household knew about my adventure; even the Princess said that I had been treated too severely. As for the Prince, I saw him, for the first time, moved to anger. He came upstairs at ten o'clock in the morning in great excitement.

'Excuse me,' he began, addressing Madame Léotard. 'What are you doing here? What a way to treat a poor child! It's barbarous, simply barbarous! Savage! A weak, sick child – such a dreamy little girl, so imaginative – and to put her alone in a dark room and leave her there all night! Why, it could kill her! Don't you know her background? It's barbaric, it's inhuman, I'm telling you, Madame! And how is such a punishment possible? Whose idea was it? Who could think up such a dreadful thing?'

Poor Madame Léotard, reduced to tears, tried, in her confusion, to explain the whole affair to him: how she had forgotten about me because of her daughter's arrival; that in itself the punishment is not a bad one if it does not go on for too long, and that Jean-Jacques Rousseau indeed spoke of something similar.

'Jean-Jacques Rousseau, Madame! But Jean-Jacques could not have said that. Jean-Jacques is no authority on the upbringing of children, he has no right. Jean-Jacques renounced his own children. Jean-Jacques was an evil man, Madame!'

'Jean-Jacques Rousseau! Jean-Jacques evil? Prince! Prince! What are you saying?' Madame Léotard was quite incensed. She was a fine woman and, above all, did not take offence easily. But to touch one of her idols, to wound the classical shades of Corneille or Racine, to insult Voltaire, to call Jean-Jacques an evil man, a barbarian ... goodness gracious! Her eyes brimmed with tears, and the poor woman was so upset that she shook from head to foot. 'You are forgetting yourself, Prince!' she said finally, beside herself with agitation.

The Prince collected himself and begged her forgiveness; then he came up to me, kissed me with great feeling, made the sign of the cross over me, and left the room.

'*Pauvre Prince!*' said Madame Léotard, who in her turn was very touched. Later, we all sat down at the school table, but the little Princess was extremely preoccupied. Before we went in to dinner, she came over to me quite flushed and, with a laugh on her lips, stopped in front of me, grabbed me by the shoulders and said hurriedly, as if ashamed of something: 'Well then, you took my punishment for me yesterday! ... Shall we go and play in the reception room after dinner?' At that moment someone walked past us, and the Princess quickly turned away from me.

After dinner, at dusk, we went downstairs to the big room, hand in hand. The little Princess was profoundly upset, and breathing heavily. I was overjoyed, happier than ever before in my life.

'Do you want to play ball?' she asked me, 'Wait here.' She stood me in a corner of the room but, instead of walking away and throwing the ball to me, she stopped after a couple of steps, glanced at me, blushed and, falling on to the sofa, buried her face in her hands. I started moving towards her; she thought I was leaving.

'Don't go, Netochka, stay with me,' she said. 'I'll be all right in a minute.' She sprang up from the sofa, flushed and tearful, and threw her arms around my neck. Her cheeks were moist, her lips as swollen as cherries, and her curls in disarray. She began kissing me wildly; my face, eyes, lips, neck and hands. She was sobbing hysterically. I clung tightly to her, and we embraced sweetly and joyfully like two lovers after a long separation. Katya's heart was racing so hard that I could hear each beat.

A voice came from the next room, summoning Katya to her mother. 'Oh, Netochka! Ah! Until this evening, until tonight! Go upstairs and wait for me.' She kissed me, sweetly, silently and fervently for the last time, and then ran off in response to Nastya's call. I ran upstairs like one resurrected from the dead, threw myself on to the sofa and, burying my head in the cushions, wept for joy. My heart was beating so hard that I felt my chest would burst, and I do not know how I survived until night-time. At last the clock struck eleven, and I went to bed. The Princess did not return till twelve; she smiled at me from the other side of the room, but said nothing. Nastya began to undress her, dawdling as if on purpose.

'Hurry, hurry! Nastya!' muttered Katya.

'What's the matter with you, Princess, you must have run all the way upstairs, your heart is beating so fast!'

'Oh, goodness, Nastya, how tedious you are! Hurry, do be quick!' said Katya, stamping her little foot on the floor in vexation.

'Ah, my dearest,' said Nastya, kissing Katya's foot as she took off the shoe.

Eventually, when her night-time preparations were complete, the Princess was put to bed, and Nastya left. She instantly leapt out of bed and rushed over to me. I cried out in greeting.

'Come here, come and lie with me,' she said, pulling me off the bed. A moment later I was in her bed, and we were embracing, hugging each other eagerly. Katya almost stifled me with her kisses.

'You see, I remember how you used to kiss me in the night!'
she said, blushing red as a poppy.

I was sobbing.

'Netochka,' whispered Katya through her tears, 'my angel,
really I've loved you for such ages, such a long time. Do you
know when it began?'

'When?'

'When Papa made me ask for forgiveness and afterwards you
stood up for your own father. Netochka . . . Oh, my little, little
orphan!' She dragged the words out, still showering kisses on
me. She was crying and laughing at the same time.

'Oh, Katya!'

'What is it? What is it?'

'Why did we wait so long . . . so long . . .' But I could not
go on. We embraced each other for three long minutes in
silence.

'Now, listen. What used you to think about me?' asked the
Princess.

'Ah! So many things, Katya! I kept thinking and thinking,
day and night.'

'And in your sleep you used to talk about me. I heard you.'

'Really?'

'I heard you crying several times.'

'No wonder! Why were you always so haughty?'

'I was the stupid one, Netochka. It just comes over me, and I
can't help it. I was so cross with you.'

'But why?'

'Because I'm so horrid. At first because I knew that you were
nicer than me, and then because Papa loves you more. But
Papa is a kind man, Netochka.'

'Oh yes!' I answered, crying as I thought about the Prince.

'A good man,' said Katya in a serious tone. 'But what am I to
do about him? He's always so . . . well . . . Ah yes, and then I
had to ask your forgiveness, and I started crying – that made
me cross again.'

'I saw that, yes, I saw that you wanted to cry.'

'Well, keep quiet, you little silly, you're a crybaby yourself!'
Katya declared, putting her hand over my mouth. 'Listen, I

really wanted to like you, and then I suddenly felt like hating you, and I loathed you, just loathed you.'

'But why?'

'I was already angry with you. I don't know why! And then I realized that you couldn't live without me, so I thought: "Now I'm going to tease her, nasty girl!" '

'Oh, Katya!'

'My darling!' said Katya, kissing my hand. 'And after that I didn't really want to talk to you, not at all. And then do you remember the time I stroked Falstaff?'

'Oh yes, you were so brave.'

'I was pet-ri-fied!' the Princess said slowly. 'And do you know why I did it?'

'Why?'

'Because you were watching me and, come what may, I had to do it. I scared you, didn't I? Weren't you afraid for me?'

'Scared to death!'

'I saw it, and I was so glad when Falstaff walked away! Good God! And I felt so frightened afterwards, when he had gone! What a mon-ster!'

The Princess burst into a nervous giggle, lifted her feverish head and began to gaze at me intently. Tears quivered like little gems on her long lashes.

'What is there about you that makes me love you so much? There you are, such a pale little thing, with your fair hair and blue eyes, and you're such a stupid crybaby ... Oh, my little orphan!' Katya leant over me again and showered kisses on me. Several tears fell on to my cheeks. She was deeply moved.

'And then, when I did begin to love you, I kept on thinking, "No, no, don't tell her." I was so afraid and ashamed – but see how lovely it is now.'

'Katya, I can't bear it!' I said, overcome with joy. 'My heart will break!'

'Come on, Netochka! Listen to me ... Listen now ... who called you Netochka?'

'Mama.'

'Will you tell me about your Mama?'

'Yes, everything, everything,' I replied in delight.

'And what have you done with my two lace handkerchiefs? And why did you take my ribbon? Shame on you! You see, I know all about it.' I laughed and blushed pitifully.

' "All right," I thought, "tease her, wait a bit." And at other times I thought, "No, I really don't love her at all, I can't stand her." And you are always so meek and mild! And I was so afraid you would think that I was silly. You're clever, Netochka, very clever, aren't you?'

'Oh, come on, Katya!' I answered, almost offended.

'No, you *are* clever,' insisted Katya, gravely and resolutely. 'I know you are. And there was one time when I got up in the morning and I loved you so terribly. I had been dreaming about you all night and I thought, "I'll go and ask Mama if I can move downstairs and sleep in her room. I don't want to love her, no I don't!" And the following night when I was falling asleep I thought: "If only she would come like last night." Well, anyway, you didn't! Oh yes, and the times when I used to pretend to be asleep . . . what shameless creatures we are, Netochka!'

'But why didn't you want to love me?'

'Because . . . I told you why, I always liked you, always! And I couldn't bear it any longer. I thought: "If I just kiss her once, I'll squeeze her to death." There now, come on, you silly thing!' And the Princess gave me a pinch.

'And do you remember the time I tied your shoelace?'

'Yes, I do.'

'I remember. And did it make you happy? I looked at you and thought, "What a sweet little thing she is; I'll go and tie her shoelace, and see what she makes of it." But I was happy too. And, you know, I really wanted to kiss you . . . but I didn't. And then it all seemed so funny, so very funny! All the time we were out walking, I kept thinking I would suddenly burst out laughing. I couldn't look at you, it was so funny. And gosh, how glad I was that you went into the dungeon and not me.' The empty room was called the dungeon. 'Were you frightened?'

'Terribly!'

'But it wasn't just that you were taking the blame that made me so happy. It was that you were ready to be punished for me. I thought: "I expect she's crying now, but how I love her!

Tomorrow I'm going to kiss her and kiss her." And actually I wasn't really so very sorry for you, even though I did cry a little.'

'But I didn't cry at all. I was frightfully happy.'

'You didn't cry? Oh, you wicked thing!' cried the Princess, pressing her lips to my neck.

'Ah, Katya, Katya, how lovely you are!'

'It's true, isn't it! Now what can I do for you? Tease me, pinch me! Keep pinching me, darling!'

'Rascal!'

'What next?'

'Silly thing.'

'Then?'

'Why kiss me!'

Crying and laughing, we kissed each other until our lips were swollen.

'Netochka, first of all you must always come and sleep in my bed. Do you like kissing? We'll kiss each other. And next, please don't be so miserable. Why were you so unhappy? Won't you tell me?'

'Yes, I'll tell you everything, but just now I'm not sad, I'm enjoying myself.'

'Your cheeks will become rosy like mine ... Oh, I hope tomorrow doesn't come too soon! ... Are you sleepy, Netochka?'

'No.'

'Then let's talk.'

We went on chatting for a couple of hours. God knows what we did not talk about. First the Princess told me all about her plans for the future, and then she explained the present state of affairs. She told me how she loved her Papa more than anyone else in the world, almost more than me. We both agreed that Madame Léotard was really quite nice and not too strict. We talked about what we might do the next day, and the day after, and all in all we settled everything for the next twenty years. Katya decided how we should live: one day she would be the one to give the orders for me to obey, and the next day I would give them to her and she would obey me unquestioningly. After that, we would take it in turns to give the orders, and if it happened that one of us refused to obey, we would argue about it, just for the sake of appearance, and then quickly make it up. In short, we looked forward to eternal happiness. Eventually we grew tired of chatting, and my eyes began to close. Katya made fun of me for being a sleepyhead, but she was the first to fall asleep. In the morning we woke up at the same time and, after a hurried kiss, I managed to scurry back into my bed before anyone came in.

All that day we were so happy we hardly knew what to do with ourselves. We kept hiding, running away from everyone, and above all avoiding meeting anyone face to face. Eventually I started telling her about my life. Katya was shocked and brought to tears by what I told her.

'Oh you naughty, naughty thing! Why didn't you tell me all this before? I would have been so kind to you, I would have loved you so much! Did those boys in the street hurt you when they hit you?'

'Yes, a lot. And I was so afraid of them!'

'Oh, the wicked things. You know, Netochka, once I saw a boy hitting another boy in the street. Tomorrow I'm going to take Falstaff's lead, and if we see one of those boys I'll give him such a beating!' Her eyes flashed in indignation.

Whenever anyone entered the room, we started, afraid of being found kissing each other, and we must have kissed each other a hundred times. So that day passed, and the following one. I thought I would die of joy; I was breathless with happiness. But our happiness did not last for long.

Madame Léotard had to report every move Katya made. She had been observing us for three days and during that time had gathered a great deal to relate. Finally she went to Katya's mother and told her everything she had noticed: that we both seemed to be in a state of frenzy; that for the last three days we had been quite inseparable; that we were continually kissing each other, laughing and crying like lunatics, and chattering incessantly; that since this had never happened before, she could not think what it could be attributed to, but she thought the Princess was undergoing some nervous crisis; and finally that she believed it would be better for us to see less of one another.

'I've been of that opinion for a long time,' answered the Princess. 'I always knew that peculiar little orphan would give us trouble. The things they told us about her, her background. Awful! Really awful! She certainly has an influence over Katya. You say that Katya loves her very much?'

'Beyond belief!'

The Princess flushed with vexation. She was beginning to feel jealous of me because of her daughter.

'It's unnatural,' she said. 'At first they seemed to avoid each other, and, I confess, I was glad of it. However young that orphan may be, I wouldn't vouch for her under any circumstances. Do you follow me? Her breeding, her habits, and possibly her morals were acquired from her mother. I can't understand what the Princess sees in her. I've suggested sending her to a boarding-school thousands of times.'

Madame Léotard attempted to defend me, but the Princess had already determined to separate us. Katya was immediately sent for, and the moment she appeared downstairs she was told that we were not to see each other until the following Sunday – in other words, for a whole week.

I learned all this late in the evening, and was aghast. I thought of Katya and could not believe that she would be able to bear our separation. I fell ill that night, overcome with grief and sorrow. In the morning the Prince came up to me and whispered something in my ear about taking heart. The Prince had done his utmost, but to no avail: the Princess refused to change her mind. I came gradually to a state of despair and found it difficult to breathe because of my misery.

On the morning of the third day, Nastya brought me a note from Katya. Penned in a terrible scrawl, it said: 'I love you very much. I am sitting here with Mama, and I keep thinking of a way of escaping and reaching you. I will escape, I've said it, so don't cry. Write and tell me how much you love me. I embraced you all night in my dreams. I am suffering terribly, Netochka. I will send you some sweets. Goodbye.'

I answered her note in the same vein and spent the day crying over Katya's note. Madame Léotard worried me with her kindness. In the evening, I discovered that she had gone to the

Prince and told him that I would certainly fall ill for the third time unless I saw Katya, and she added that she regretted having spoken to the Princess. I questioned Nastya about Katya. She told me that she was not crying, but that she was dreadfully pale.

In the morning Nastya whispered to me: 'Go to his excellency's study. Go by the staircase on the right.' I suddenly came alive again with anticipation. Panting, I ran downstairs and opened the door to his study. She was not there. Then Katya grabbed me from behind and kissed me passionately. Laughter, tears ... In a flash she broke away from my embrace and climbed up on to her father's knees, then on to his shoulders, just like a squirrel. But she lost her balance and bounced down again on to the sofa. The Prince fell down after her. She was crying with delight.

'Oh, Papa! What a good man you are, Papa!'

'You little imps! What has happened to you both? What kind of a friendship is this? What sort of love?'

'Be quiet, Papa, you don't understand our affairs.' And we rushed into each other's arms.

I began to look more closely at Katya. She had grown thinner in those three days. Her healthy glow had faded from her little face, and a pallor had taken its place. It made me so sad that I started to cry. Finally, Nastya knocked at the door: this was a sign that Katya had been missed and they were asking for her. Katya turned as pale as death.

'Enough, children,' said the Prince. 'We'll meet together every day. Goodbye, and God bless you.' He was moved by the sight of us, but his words did not come true. The same evening, news came that little Sasha had suddenly fallen ill and was almost on the point of death. The Princess decided to set off the following day. This happened so abruptly that I knew nothing about it until the very moment of saying farewell to Katya. It was the Prince who had insisted on these goodbyes, the Princess being very reluctant to agree. Katya was heartbroken. I ran downstairs, hardly knowing what I was doing, and rushed to embrace her. The travelling coach was already standing at the front door. When she saw me, Katya uttered a scream and fainted. I rushed to kiss her. Her mother was trying to revive her. At last, she regained consciousness and embraced me again.

'Goodbye, Netochka!' she said to me quickly, half-smiling, with the strangest expression on her face. 'Don't mind me. It's nothing, I'm not ill. I'll be back again in a month, and then we won't ever part again.'

'Enough,' said the Princess calmly. 'Let's go now.'

But the little Princess came back once more and squeezed me convulsively in her arms.

'My life!' she managed to whisper as she hugged me, 'good-bye.' We kissed each other for the last time, and then the little Princess vanished, for a long, long time. Eight years passed before we met again.

I have related this childhood episode in detail on purpose; it was the first appearance of Katya in my life. But our stories are inseparable: her romance was my romance. It seems that I was destined to meet her, and she was destined to find me. Besides, I could not deny myself the pleasure of being carried away once more by childhood memories ... Now my story moves faster. My life at this point fell into a period of tranquillity, and only when I was sixteen did I wake up again.

But first, a few words about what happened to me after the Prince's family departed for Moscow.

I was left with Madame Léotard. Two weeks after their departure, a courier arrived, informing us that the return to Petersburg was postponed indefinitely. As Madame Léotard could not go to Moscow, owing to family circumstances, her service in the Prince's house was at an end. However, she did remain with the family, entering the home of the Princess's elder daughter, Alexandra Mikhailovna.

I have said nothing yet about Alexandra Mikhailovna, and indeed I had only seen her once. She was the daughter of the Princess by her first husband. The origin and family connections of the Princess were rather obscure. Her first husband had been merely a leaseholder. When the Princess remarried, she did not know what to do with her elder daughter. There was little hope of a brilliant match, for her dowry was a modest one. At last, four years before I arrived, they had succeeded in marrying her to a man who was both wealthy and of significant rank. Alexandra Mikhailovna found herself in an altogether new world, passing in very different circles of society. The Princess used to visit her twice a year; the Princess, her step-father, visited her every week, taking Katya with him. Lately, however, the Princess had been reluctant to let Katya visit her sister, and so the Prince had taken her secretly. Katya adored her sister, but they could not have had more dissimilar characters. Alexandra Mikhailovna was a woman of twenty-two; she was quiet, gentle and loving. But some secret sorrow, some hidden heartache seemed to cast a shadow of austerity over her beautiful features. Sternness and gravity were no more compatible with the angelic serenity of her face than with that of a child. One could not look at her without feeling the deepest sympathy. The first time I saw her, she was extremely pale – she was said to be prone to tuberculosis. She led a very reclusive, almost monastic existence, and she had no interest in social occasions, whether in her own home or elsewhere. She had no children at this time. I remember she came to see Madame Léotard and came up to me, kissing me warmly. She was accompanied by a thin, rather elderly man. He was the violinist B. When he saw me, he shed a few tears. Alexandra Mikhailovna put her arms around me and asked me whether I would like to come and live with her as her daughter. Looking into her face, I recognized my Katya's sister, and I embraced her with a dull pain in my heart which made my whole chest throb. It was as if once again I was hearing someone saying: 'Little orphan.' Later, Alexandra Mikhailovna showed me a letter from the Prince. In it were a few lines addressed to me, and I had to stifle my sobs while reading them. The Prince gave me his blessing, wished me a long life of happiness and begged me to love his other daughter. Katya also added a few lines, telling me that she would not leave her mother now.

And so, that evening, I entered into another family, another home, with new people. Once again I had to tear myself away from all that had grown dear to me and to which I felt I belonged. I arrived completely exhausted, and racked with mental suffering . . . Now a new story begins.

CHAPTER SIX

My new life was as serene and peaceful as if I had settled among hermits ... I lived for more than eight years with my new guardians, and in all that time I recall only a very few occasions when there were evening parties, dinners or gatherings of friends or relatives ... With the exception of two or three people who visited from time to time, the musician B., who was a friend of the family, and the people who came to see Alexandra Mikhailovna's husband, usually on business, no one ever came to the house.

Alexandra Mikhailovna's husband was constantly occupied with his business affairs and with official duties, and could seldom manage to find even a little free time; when he did, it was divided equally between his family and his social life. Important connections, which he could not ignore, necessitated his making frequent appearances in society. There were widespread rumours about his boundless ambition; but as he held an extremely prominent position and had the reputation of being a serious and businesslike man who seemed to find luck and success everywhere, public opinion was far from denying him its approval. On the contrary, people always showed a special liking for him, which they never extended to his wife. Alexandra Mikhailovna lived in complete isolation, but she seemed to be glad of it. Her gentle nature seemed to have been created for seclusion.

She was devoted to me with her whole heart, loving me as if I had been her own daughter, and – with my eyes still moist from parting with Katya, and with an aching heart – I threw myself eagerly into the maternal embrace of my benefactress. From that time, my warm love for her was never interrupted. She was a mother to me, and a friend and a sister; she replaced the whole world for me, and she fostered my youth. Moreover, I soon perceived intuitively that her lot was by no means as rosy as might have been imagined at first sight from her quiet and apparently calm life, from her air of freedom, from the placid, bright smile which so often shone on her face. As I grew up, every day I discovered new things about the life of my benefactress, things which my heart slowly and painfully surmised, and alongside this sorrowful recognition my devotion to her grew greater and greater.

She had a gentle, frail nature. To look at her clear, peaceful features, it would have been hard to imagine that any worries could trouble her noble being. It was unthinkable that she could dislike anyone; compassion was always uppermost in her heart, prevailing even over repulsion. Yet she had very few close friends, and lived in almost complete solitude . . . She was by nature passionate and impressionable; it was as if she were constantly guarding her heart, not allowing it to forget itself, not even in dreams. Sometimes, even in her brightest moments, I noticed tears in her eyes as though a sudden, painful memory of something which troubled her conscience had flared up in her soul; as if something was watching over her happiness and seeking to upset it. And it seemed as though the happier she was, the calmer and more tranquil her life, the closer she was to this depression, and the more likely was the appearance of sudden melancholy and the tears of a nervous collapse. I cannot recall a single undisturbed month during those eight years. Her husband appeared to be very fond of her; she worshipped him. But from the first it seemed as if there was something unspoken between them. There was some secret in their life; I always suspected this.

Alexandra Mikhailovna's husband made a gloomy impression on me from the outset. This impression, formed in my childhood, was never forgotten. In appearance he was tall and slim, and seemed deliberately to conceal his gaze behind large green spectacles. He was cold and taciturn, with little to say, even in private conversation with his wife. He evidently found people very tiresome. He paid no attention to me whatsoever, and consequently, on the occasions when we all three met for tea in the drawing-room, I always felt ill at ease. As I glanced stealthily at Alexandra Mikhailovna, I would be distressed to see that she seemed to hesitate over every move she made. She would turn pale if she noticed her husband was being sterner or more depressed than usual; she would suddenly blush all over if she heard or suspected an edge in something he said. I sensed that she found it awkward to be with him, yet, to all appearances, she could not live without him for one minute. I was struck by her exceptional devotion to his every need, his every word and gesture; it was as if she wished from the depth of her heart to find a way of pleasing him and yet knew she had no hope of success. She seemed to beg his approval: the slightest smile on his face, the least word of tenderness, and she was happy, as if those were the exact moments of the beginning of a completely timorous, hopeless love. She tended to her husband's needs as if he were gravely ill.

When he left her to go to his study, he would give her hand a disdainful squeeze, after which she would change completely. Her conversation would become more cheerful, and she would move more freely. Nevertheless, there was a certain awkwardness that always came over her after each encounter with her husband. She would start going over everything he had said, weighing each word. It was not unusual for her to turn to me and ask whether she had heard him correctly: was it this that Pyotr Alexandrovitch had meant? She seemed to be searching for another meaning in his words. It might take a full hour for her to regain her assurance, to persuade herself that he was pleased with her and that she had no cause for anxiety. Then she would again become affectionate, cheerful and happy: she would start laughing and kissing me, and might improvise on the piano for an hour or more. But, more often than not, her happiness was shortlived: she would suddenly start crying and, when I saw her troubled embarrassment and fright, would quickly assure me, in a whisper, as if she were afraid of being overheard, that her tears meant nothing, that she was quite happy, and that I need not worry about her. There were also times when in her husband's absence, she suddenly became nervous, and would start inquiring after him. She would send someone to find out what he was doing, would start asking the maids why orders had been given to harness the horses, where he was intending to go, whether he was unwell, cheerful or melancholy, what he had said, and so on. She never dared initiate a conversation with him about his interests or business affairs. Whenever he offered her advice or asked her about anything, she listened timidly, as self-consciously as if she were his slave. She was absolutely delighted if he happened to praise anything of hers: a book, her sewing, anything at all. It seemed to make her feel proud and instantly happier. But she would be made truly ecstatic on those occasions (very rare) when he took it into his head to fondle one of their two small children. Her face would be transformed with joy, and sometimes she would show too much fondness to her husband. For instance, she might be bold enough to suggest, without encouragement from him, and with a certain degree of trepidation and in a faltering voice, that he might listen to a new piece of music that she had just received, or that he might give his opinion of a new book. She sometimes went as far as to ask him to read a page or two of something that had particularly impressed her that day. On occasion her husband magnanimously fulfilled these requests, smiling with condescension, as one smiles on a spoilt child, afraid of denying the satisfaction of some strange whim, for fear of crudely spoiling its naïvety too soon. I do not know why, but I resisted that smile with my whole being; and I resented his supercilious condescension and the inequality between them. I kept quiet, restraining myself and observing them with my childlike curiosity and prematurely harsh criticism. At other times I noticed that she would seem startled, as if involuntarily recalling something painful, dreadful and inevitable. His condescending smile would disappear, and he would fix his gaze on his intimidated wife with a look so compassionate that it made me wince. I realize now that if that look had been directed at me I would have found it intolerable. At these moments, all the joy vanished from Alexandra Mikhailovna's face, and the music recital or the reading would be interrupted. She would turn pale and, restraining herself, keep silent. There might follow an awkward, depressing moment; at times it seemed to go on for ever. It was always her husband who brought it to an end. He

would rise from his chair, struggling to suppress his agitation
and annoyance, then walk to and fro several times in sullen
silence, press his wife by the hand, heave a deep sigh and, with
obvious embarrassment, mutter a few abrupt words which
might have indicated a wish to comfort her, and then leave the
room. Alexandra Mikhailovna was either reduced to tears or fell
into a terrible, prolonged melancholy. Frequently, when he took
his leave of her in the evening, he blessed her, making the sign
of the cross over her as if she were a child. She would receive
the blessing with reverence and gratitude.

I cannot forget certain evenings in that house (two or three
only in those eight years) when Alexandra Mikhailovna seemed
suddenly transformed. Anger and indignation were reflected in
her usually gentle face, replacing her invariable self-abasement
and adoration of her husband. Sometimes the storm would be
gathering for a whole hour; her husband would become more
silent, austere and surly than usual. At last, the poor woman's
wounded heart would be able to bear it no more. In a voice
breaking with emotion, she would begin talking, at first hesitantly, disconnectedly, with hints and bitter pauses; then, as if
unable to endure her anguish, she would burst into tears and
sobs, and there would follow an outburst of indignation, of
reproaches, of complaints, of despair, as though she were
having a nervous crisis. It was astonishing to see with what
patience her husband would bear it, with what sympathy he
would bend down to comfort her, kiss her hands, and even at
last begin weeping with her; then she would seem to recollect
herself, her conscience would apparently cry out and convict
her. Her husband's tears shattered her. She would wring her
hands in despair and, with convulsive sobs, fall at his feet and
beg the forgiveness that would be immediately granted her. But
the agonies of her conscience, the tears and supplications for
forgiveness would go on for a long time, and she would be still
more nervous, still more timid in his presence, for whole
months. I could understand nothing of these reproaches and
upbraidings; I was sent out of the room on such occasions,
always very awkwardly. But they could not keep their secret
from me entirely. I watched, I noticed, I divined certain things,

and from the beginning a vague suspicion arose in me that some mystery lay at the bottom of it all, that these sudden outbursts of an exasperated heart were not simply caused by nerves; that there was some reason for her husband always being sullen; that there was some reason for his double-edged compassion for his poor sick wife; that there was some reason for her everlasting timidity before him, and for this quiet, strange love which she dared not reveal to her husband. There must be some cause for her isolation, for her reclusive existence, and for those blushes and the sudden deathly pallor that appeared on her face when she was with her husband.

But, since such scenes were very rare; since life was very monotonous, and I was really too close to her to observe her; since I was developing and growing very rapidly, and many new things were beginning to awaken inside me (albeit subconsciously), diverting me from such observations, I at last grew accustomed to the life, habits and people around me. I could not, of course, help wondering at times, as I looked at Anna Mikhailovna, but as yet my doubts had reached no conclusion. I loved her very much, respected her sadness and was afraid of troubling her vulnerable heart with my curiosity. She understood me and was often prepared to thank me for my devotion! Sometimes, noticing my concern, she would smile through her tears and laugh at her own tendency to cry; then she would suddenly begin telling me that she was very contented, very happy, that everyone was so kind to her, that everyone she had ever known had been fond of her, that she was very distressed that Pyotr Alexandrovitch was always so worried about her, and about her peace of mind, when really she was, on the contrary, so happy, so happy ...

And then she would embrace me with such deep feeling, with so much love written on her face, that my heart, if I may say so, nearly bled with sympathy for her.

Her features have never faded from my memory. They were symmetrical, and their thinness and pallor only accentuated the austere charm of her beauty. Her thick black hair, combed smoothly down, framed her cheeks in sharp, severe outline, making a lovely contrast to her soft gaze. Her large, childishly clear blue eyes at times reflected so much simplicity and timidity that they seemed defenceless, as if fearful of every sensation, every outburst of emotion, every momentary joy and frequent quiet sorrow. Yet at certain happy, untroubled moments, there was much that was serene and bright as day, so much goodness and calm in the heart-piercing glance. Her eyes, blue as the heavens, radiated so much love and warmth, so much profound sympathy for all that was noble, for everything that asked for love and begged compassion, that one's soul surrendered entirely to her; it seemed to be involuntarily drawn to her and to catch from her the same serenity, the same calm spirit and reconciliatory love. In the same way, one might look up at the blue sky and feel ready to spend whole hours in secret contemplation, bringing freedom and tranquillity to the soul, as if the lofty cupola of the heavens were reflected in the skies like a still sheet of water. When – and this often happened – exaltation sent the colour rushing to her cheeks and her bosom heaved with emotion, her eyes would flash like lightning, seeming to give off sparks, as if her whole soul, which had been chastely guarding the pure flame of beauty, was now illuminating her and passing into her eyes. At these moments she was like a being inspired. And in this sudden rush of inspiration, in this transition from a mood of shrinking gentleness to heightened spiritual exaltation, to pure stern enthusiasm, there flowed simultaneously so much that was childishly impulsive, so much childlike faith, that I believe an artist would have given half his life to portray one such moment of lofty ecstasy and put that inspired face on canvas.

From my earliest days in that house, I noticed that she was delighted to welcome me into her solitary existence. She had only one child at that time, and had been a mother for only twelve months. But I was just like a daughter to her, and she could not make any distinction between me and her own children. With what fervour she set about my education! She was in such a hurry in the beginning that Madame Léotard could not help smiling as she watched her. Indeed, we tried to do everything so precipitately that we could not understand each other. She started teaching me herself, but she tried to do too much at once, which resulted in ever more zeal, fervour and devoted patience on her part rather than in any real benefit to me. At first she was disappointed by her lack of success, but we laughed it off and started again from the beginning, although Alexandra Mikhailovna still, in spite of her initial failures, boldly declared herself opposed to Madame Léotard's system. They argued cordially, but my new teacher was absolutely against any system, and insisted that we should find the correct method as we went along and that it was pointless to fill my head with dry information, for success depended on understanding my instincts and on the ability to arouse my goodwill – and she was right, for she had a complete victory. From the beginning, the usual pupil–teacher relationship vanished entirely. We studied like two friends, and sometimes it seemed as if I was teaching Alexandra Mikhailovna, without her noticing the crafty shift. And arguments often arose between us: I would become vehement in trying to prove my point, while Alexandra Mikhailovna would imperceptibly lead me the right way. But it would end in our reaching the truth we were pursuing, and then I would detect the stratagem and, thinking about all the effort she made for me, frequently sacrificing whole hours in this way for my benefit, I could only throw my arms around her neck and hug her.

She was astonished and moved by my sensitivity. She began showing interest in my past, wanting to hear of it from my own mouth, and every time I told her something she would grow more tender and serious with me – more serious because, through my unhappy childhood, I aroused in her both compassion and a feeling of something approaching respect. After my confessions, we usually fell into long conversations, during which she explained my past to me in such a way that I really seemed to live through it again, and I learnt a great deal that was new. Madame Léotard often thought such talk too serious and, seeing my involuntary tears, thought them quite unsuitable. I thought the very opposite, for after such 'lessons' I felt as lighthearted and happy as if there had been no misfortune in my life. Moreover, I was terribly grateful to Alexandra Mikhailovna for making me love her more and more every day.

Madame Léotard had no idea of the way in which everything that had hitherto risen up in my soul, so inadvertently, like some premature storm, was now being smoothed out and brought into harmony. She had no idea that my childish heart had been torn to shreds, tortured with pain so cruelly unfair that it had cried out with anguish, without understanding the source of these pangs ...

The day began with our meeting in the baby's nursery; we woke him, washed him, dressed him, fed him, played with him and taught him to talk. At length, we would leave the baby and sit down to study. We studied a great deal, but they were strange lessons. There was everything in them, but nothing precise. We read, exchanged ideas, put aside the book and turned to music, without noticing the hours flying by. In the evenings B., who was a friend of Alexandra Mikhailovna, would come and, together with Madame Léotard, join us in the most fervid, passionate conversations on art, life (which was known to our little circle only by hearsay), reality, ideals, the past, the future; we would sit up beyond midnight. I listened as hard as I could, shared the enthusiasm of the others, laughed and was moved. It was at this time that I learnt in detail all about my father and my early childhood. Meanwhile I was growing up: teachers were hired for me, from whom I would have learnt nothing were it not for Alexandra Mikhailovna. With my Geography teacher I would simply have gone blind as I searched for cities and rivers on the maps. With Alexandra Mikhailovna we set off on such voyages, visiting such countries, seeing so many marvellous sights and experiencing so many magical and fantastic hours! Our zeal was so strong that we ran out of books and had to find new ones. Before long, I could point out things to the Geography teacher myself – although, in fairness to him, he always maintained his superiority in respect of his precise knowledge of the latitude and longitude in which any given city lay, as well as the exact population in thousands, hundreds and tens. The History teacher was also paid a regular fee, but when he had left, Alexandra Mikhailovna and I studied History in our own way; we turned to books and were sometimes so absorbed in what we were doing that we read on deep into the night, or rather Alexandra Mikhailovna read on, for she also censored the material. I never felt so enthusiastic as after these readings. We were both excited, as if we ourselves were the heroes. Of course, we read more between the lines than was there, and besides, Alexandra Mikhailovna was so clever at describing things that it seemed as if all she read about had really happened to her. It may perhaps seem amusing that we became so excited and stayed up after midnight, I a mere child and she a stricken heart, burdened with the troubles of life! I knew that she found it restful to be beside me. I remember sometimes becoming exceptionally thoughtful as I gazed at her. Even before I had actually begun to live, I had fathomed a great deal about life.

At last I was thirteen. In the meanwhile Alexandra Mikhailovna's health had grown steadily worse. She had become increasingly irritable, and her attacks of melancholy and despair were more severe. Her husband's visits became more frequent, and he used to sit with her, but, as before, he did not speak and was stern and gloomy for long periods. I became more intensely concerned about her lot. I was growing out of childhood, and a wealth of new impressions, observations, interests and surmises were forming inside me. I was increasingly tormented by the enigma that surrounded the family. There were moments when I thought I had some kind of understanding of the problem. At other times, finding no solution to my questions, I lapsed into indifference, apathy, even annoyance, and my curiosity waned. In the course of time, I experienced a curious need (and this became ever more frequent), to be alone and to think, to do nothing but think. It was a period not dissimilar to that when I was still living with my parents but before I had grown close to my father, when, for an entire year, I had brooded and fantasized as I peered out of the window from my little corner, until I became like a wild creature lost in the fancies of my own creation. The difference now was that I was less patient, I grieved more, new unconscious impulses arose within me, and I had more thirst for activity and excitement. I could no longer concentrate on one thing, as I had been able to before. And

Alexandra Mikhailovna seemed to be withdrawing from me more and more. At my age, it was scarcely possible to be her friend. Though I was not a child, I asked too many questions and often looked at her in such a way that she lowered her eyes. These were strange moments. I could not bear to see her in tears, and often just to look at her brought tears to my own eyes. I would throw my arms around her and hug her fervently. What answer could she give me? I felt that I was a burden to her. But at other times (and these were sad and difficult moments), it was she who embraced me violently and desperately, as if seeking my sympathy, as if unable to bear her loneliness. Perhaps she felt that I understood her and suffered with her. But it was, nevertheless, clear that there was a secret standing between us, and I began to avoid her during such periods. I found it awkward to be with her and, besides, there was now little that brought us together, apart from music. But her doctor had forbidden music. Books? That was even more difficult, since she was at a loss to know what to read with me. We never got beyond the first page; she found a possible hidden meaning in every word, in every insignificant paragraph. We both avoided intimate or sincere conversations.

It was just at this time that fate, in the strangest and most extraordinary manner, altered my life, brusquely and unexpectedly. All my attention, my heart, my mind and my soul were suddenly, with great intensity and fervour, directed towards a new, unforeseeable activity; without really becoming aware of it, I was carried away to another world. I had no time to turn back, to look round, or to change my mind. Although I felt I might be on the path to my downfall, temptation proved stronger than my fear, and I closed my eyes and went ahead without thinking. Then, for a long time, I was diverted from the reality which had begun to weigh on me, and from which I had so eagerly and helplessly sought an escape. This is what happened.

There were three doors leading out of the dining-room: one to the drawing-rooms, one to the nursery and my room, and the other one to the library. There was also another passage from the library, separated from my room by a study where

128

Pyotr Alexandrovitch's secretary, a man who served as both copyist and administrator, was usually occupied with business correspondence. The key to the library and the bookcases was kept in his room. One day, after dinner, when he was not in the house, I discovered the key lying on the floor. Eaten up with curiosity and armed with my find, I entered the library. It was a rather large, very light room with eight huge bookcases filled with books. There were a great number of books, most of which had come to Pyotr Alexandrovitch by inheritance. The remainder had been collected by Alexandra Mikhailovna, who was continually buying them. Up until now, great care had been taken in the choice of books I was given to read, and it was not difficult for me to guess that there was much that was forbidden, kept secret from me. That was why I opened the first bookcase and took out the first book with irresistible curiosity, with a rush of terror and excitement and a peculiar, unaccountable feeling. The bookcase was full of novels. I took one of them, shut the bookcase, and took the book off to my room with such a strange sensation and with such throbbing and fluttering of the heart that it was as if I foresaw that a great transformation was going to take place in my life. I went into my room, locked the door and opened the book. But I could not read it, for my mind was preoccupied with other things: I had to plan my access to the library securely, once and for all, and in such a way that no one would know. I wished to continue to be able to get any book at any time, and so I postponed my pleasure until a more appropriate moment; I took the book back, but hid the key in my room. Hiding that key was the first evil action in my life. I awaited the results; they were most satisfactory: Pyotr Alexandrovitch's secretary, after spending an entire evening and most of the night on his knees, candle in hand, searching for the key, decided in the morning to send for a locksmith. The latter came, bringing with him a bunch of keys, among which was one that fitted the library door. There the matter rested, and nothing more was said about the lost key. I was so cautious that I did not go into the library until a week later, when I felt certain that there was no risk of arousing suspicion. At first I chose a time of day when the secretary was not at home; afterwards I took to going into the library from the dining-room, for Pyotr Alexandrovitch's secretary always kept the key in his pocket and, having only an indirect concern with the books, never went into the room where they were kept.

I began reading avidly, and soon I was entirely absorbed in the books. All my new cravings, my recent ambitions, the still vague impulses of my adolescence and the restlessness induced by precocious development (all of which disturbed my soul so badly) suddenly found a new outlet. It all happened very rapidly, and I admit to being most pleased with the newly discovered sustenance. Soon my heart and my mind were so enchanted, and my imagination was developing so widely, that I seemed to forget the whole world which had surrounded me until then. It seemed as though fate itself had brought me to the threshold of this new life, for which I was so enthusiastic, and about which I dreamt day and night; as though, before letting me step on to the unknown path, it had led me up on to a height, showing me the future in a magic panorama, in dazzling and alluring perspective. I was destined to live through that future by getting to know it first in books, experiencing it in dreams, in hopes, in passionate impulses, in the sweet emotions of a youthful spirit. I began reading at random, picking up the first book that fell into my hands, but fate was watching over me. What I had discovered and lived through until that time was so noble, so austere, that no evil or impure page could attract me. I was guarded by my childish instinct, my youth and my past. It was now that consciousness, all at once, seemed to illuminate the whole of my past life. Indeed, almost every page I read seemed already familiar, as if I had lived it all long ago; the passions, the enchanting pictures, life portrayed in such unfamiliar forms, was already familiar to me. It fascinated me, making me oblivious of the present, almost alienating me from reality; in every book I read, I found embodied the laws of the same fatality, the same spirit of adventure which commands the lives of each individual, yet is derived from some basic law of human life, which is the condition of salvation, preservation and happiness. I exerted all my strength and intuition in order to understand this law, of which I had but a glimmering and which had roused a feeling rather like self-preservation inside me. It was as if I had been forewarned, as though someone were prompting me. It seemed some prophecy was gripping my heart. And every day hope grew stronger and stronger in my heart, and my yearnings, too, grew greater; yearnings for that future, for that sort of life about which I read every day, and which struck me with such artistic force and poetic fascination. However, as I have already said, my fantasies prevailed over my impatience, and indeed it was only in dreams that I was so bold, while in reality I was instinctively nervous of the future. And so, as if by previous agreement with myself, I unconsciously decided to be content for the time being with the world of dreams in which I alone was the master, and in which there was only temptation and joy, while misfortune, if admitted at all, played only a passive, transient role, essential for the sake of contrast and for the sudden turn of destiny that was to give a happy solution to the ecstatic romances in my brain. That is how I interpret now my state of mind at that time.

And to think that this kind of life, a life of the imagination, a life absolutely divorced from my surroundings, could last for three whole years!

This life was my secret, and even at the end of those three years I did not know whether to be in dread of its sudden discovery. All that I had lived through in those three years was too intimate, too close to me. I was myself too distinctly reflected in those fantasies, so much so that in the end I might have been frightened and confused had anyone, no matter who, cast an indiscreet glance into my soul. Moreover, every member of the house lived in such seclusion, such isolation from society, such cloistered stillness, that we had to develop an inner life of our own, a place of retreat. That was what happened to me. Nothing around me changed during those three years; everything remained as before. A depressing monotony prevailed, and when I think about it now I feel sure that if I had not immersed myself in my secret, hidden life, my soul would have been so tormented that I would have resorted to some unknown and dangerous path of escape from that spiritless and miserable circle – a path that might, perhaps, have led to my ruin. Madame Léotard had grown older and was almost always locked away in her room; the two children were still too young; B. never changed; and Alexandra Mikhailovna's husband was as severe, unapproachable and self-absorbed as ever. Between him and his wife, the same mysterious relationship still persisted, and it took on an increasingly sinister and forbidding aspect in my imagination. I became ever more afraid for Alexandra Mikhailovna. Her life, joyless and colourless, was being extinguished before my eyes. Her health grew worse by the day, and at last she seemed to give up hope. She was weighed down by something mysterious, indefinable, which she could not account for; by something which, though it was incomprehensible to her, she accepted as the inevitable cross of her condemned life. In the end, this ghastly torment embittered her; even her intelligence took another direction, dark and melancholy. One thing I observed struck me particularly: it seemed to me that, as I grew older, she held herself more aloof from me, so much so that her reserve with me turned into a sort of impatient annoyance. At certain moments she actually gave the impression of disliking me and made me feel that I was in her way. As I have said, I purposely took to avoiding her and, once away from her, I became infected by the secretiveness of her character. That was why all that I lived through during those three years, all that was taking shape in my soul, in my dreams, hopes, thoughts and passionate delights, was obstinately kept to myself. Having once started to conceal things from one another, we never became close again, although I still believed that I loved her more and more each day. I cannot recall without tears how devoted she was to me, how she used to lavish all the loving treasures her heart possessed upon me, and to the very end she fulfilled her promise of being a mother to me. It is true that her own sorrow sometimes distracted her attention for long periods, and she would appear to have forgotten about me, all the more so since I tried to distract all attention from myself; as my sixteenth birthday approached, no one seemed aware of it. But in her moments of lucidity, when she took a clear view of what was going on around her, Alexandra Mikhailovna would suddenly seem troubled about me; she would anxiously summon me from my room, would shower questions upon me about my lessons and my pursuits (testing me, as it were, examining me), and would not part with me for days. She would guess all my hopes and desires, evidently concerned about my age, about my present and my future development. With inexhaustible love, and even with a certain respect, she tried to help me. But by then she was so out of touch with me that I often found her efforts naïve and obvious to me. For instance (this happened when I was sixteen), she interrupted me one day to ask what I was reading and seemed to take fright on learning that I had not yet progressed beyond the childish books suitable for a girl of twelve. I guessed her feelings and watched her attentively.

For the next two weeks she seemed to be preparing and testing me, trying to determine the extent of my development and needs. At last she decided to make a start: Sir Walter Scott's novel *Ivanhoe* appeared on my table – a book I had long since read, at least three times. Initially she studied my reactions with timid expectation, measuring them apprehensively. At last the constraint between us, of which I was well aware, vanished; we both grew excited, and I felt so happy, so overjoyed, that I no longer had to hide from her. By the time we had finished the novel, she was delighted with me. Every observation I made during the reading session was true, every impression was correct. In her eyes, my development was already tremendous. She was so delighted with me that, in her elation, and because she wished to end the separation from me, she was prepared to undertake the supervision of my education again; but this was not within her power. Fate soon divided us, preventing us from being close friends again. The first attack of illness, the first bout of her interminable depression, was sufficient to do this; again there were estrangements, secrets, mistrustfulness, perhaps even embitterment.

Yet even at such times, there were moments outside our control. When we read together, a few kind sentences would be exchanged between us; or when we studied some music, we would soon forget ourselves and speak freely – sometimes too freely, making us ill at ease afterwards. Realizing what was happening, we would look at one another in dismay, full of suspicion and curiosity. We both had a limit to the intimacy we could allow ourselves, beyond which we dared not go, however much we might wish it.

One evening, just before dusk, I was dreaming over a book in Alexandra Mikhailovna's sitting-room. She was at the piano, improvising on a theme from one of her favourite Italian operas. When she reached the pure melody of the aria, I found myself so captivated and roused by the music that I began timidly, in a soft voice, to hum the tune to myself. I was soon carried away and got up to go over to the piano. As if she had been expecting this, Alexandra Mikhailovna began playing the accompaniment, sensitively following every note as I sang. She seemed to be astounded by the richness of my voice. I had never before sung in her presence, and I myself hardly knew whether or not I had any talent for singing. Now we both became inspired; my voice continued to rise, and I was stirred to greater energy and passion, intensified by Alexandra Mikhailovna's delighted wonder, which I could perceive in every touch of her accompaniment. The song ended successfully, with so much spirit and power that she seized my hand in delight and gazed at me joyfully.

'Annetta, you have a simply wonderful voice!' she said. 'My goodness! How is it I haven't noticed it before?'

'I've only just noticed it myself,' I replied, beside myself with joy.

'God bless you, my dear sweet child. Be thankful to Him for the gift. Who knows ... Oh, my goodness, my goodness!' She was stunned by this unexpected event, and in such a state of ecstatic happiness that she did not know what to say to me or how to lavish enough praise on me. It was one of those moments of revelation, of empathy and closeness, such as we had known before. An hour later, it was as if the whole household was celebrating a festival. B. was sent for immediately, and while we awaited his arrival we happened to discover another piece of music that was more familiar to me, and I launched into the aria. This time I was trembling nervously. I did not want to ruin the first impression with a failure, but my voice soon gathered strength, and I gained courage. I myself was astonished by the strength of my voice and, during this second experiment, all doubts vanished. In her impetuous joy, Alexandra Mikhailovna sent for her children and their nurse, and was even so bold as to call her husband from his study, which as a rule she would hardly have dreamt of doing. Pyotr Alexandrovitch received her news graciously, congratulated me and was the first to insist that I be given singing lessons. Alexandra Mikhailovna was overwhelmed with gratitude; it was as if something unbelievable had been done for her, and she rushed to kiss his hand. At last, B. appeared. The old man was overjoyed. He was very fond of me. He used to talk of my father and of the past, and when I had sung before him two or three times he announced, gravely, anxiously, and perhaps even a little mysteriously, that undoubtedly I had a voice, possibly even talent, and that it was out of the question to leave me untrained. Then, as if on second thoughts, Alexandra Mikhailovna and he agreed that it was risky to praise me too much at the beginning. I could see them exchanging glances and plotting together on the sly, which made their whole conspiracy against me extremely naïve and awkward. I sang again, and saw them trying to restrain themselves, then going out of their way to point out my defects; this made me laugh for the rest of the evening. But they did not keep it up for long. Once again B. displayed his delight. I had never suspected him of being so fond of me. The evening was spent in warm, friendly conversation. B. told the stories of several celebrated singers and musicians, speaking with the enthusiasm of an artist, with reverence and feeling. In the course of the conversation he touched on my father, and then moved on to me and my childhood, to Prince X., and to his family, of whom I had heard so little since our separation. Alexandra Mikhailovna did not know much about them herself. Since he often went to Moscow, B. knew the most. At this point the conversation took a mysterious, puzzling turn; one or two things were said about Prince X. which made no sense to me. Alexandra Mikhailovna spoke of Katya, but B. could tell us nothing in particular about her, indeed he gave the impression of being very reluctant to talk about her. I was surprised by this. Not only had I not forgotten Katya, not only was I still immersed in my former love for her, but it was quite inconceivable to me that she could have changed even in the slightest degree. The effect of our separation, the number of years that had passed during which there had been no communication between us, the differences in our upbringing and characters, had all escaped my notice. After all, in my mind, Katya had never left me. She still seemed to live inside me, especially in all my dreams, in all the romances and adventures of my fantasies, where the two of us always went hand in hand, inseparable. I imagined myself to be the heroine of every novel I read, and I always found a place in the story for Katya, my friend and Princess. Every novel had two parts, one of which was created by me, shamelessly borrowing from my favourite authors.

The family council finally decided to engage a singing teacher for me. B. recommended the best and most famous one, and the following day D., an Italian, appeared. After listening to me, he agreed with his friend B. and insisted that I would gain the best benefit by going to him for lessons where I could study with his other pupils and where the competition, the chance to emulate, and the wealth of resources at my disposal would be advantageous to the development of my voice. Alexandra Mikhailovna gave her consent, and thereafter, at eight in the morning, three days a week, I would set off for the conservatoire, escorted by one of the servants.

I shall now relate a strange happening which had a decisive effect on me and which marked a quick transition in my development. I had just reached sixteen when I was overcome with an unbearable, depressing lethargy which I could not understand. All my fantasies and enthusiasms subsided, my daydreaming waned from lack of energy, and my former youthful fervour was replaced by cold indifference. Even my talent, about which all those dearest to me had been so enthusiastic, lost its interest for me, and I ignored it listlessly. Nothing seemed to divert me; my impassivity extended even to Alexandra Mikhailovna, and for this I reproached myself, since I was actually conscious of it. My apathy was interrupted now and then by unpredictable sorrow and tears. Once again I sought solitude. At that strange period, one particular event shook me to the depth of my being and transformed the dead calm into a real tempest. My heart was bitterly wounded. This is what happened.

CHAPTER SEVEN

I went into the library (it is a moment that I shall always remember) and took a novel of Sir Walter Scott's, *St Ronan's Well*, the only one of his works I had not already read. I remember that a bitter, indefinite misery made my heart ache, as if in foreboding. I wanted to cry. There was a bright light in the room from the slanting rays of the setting sun, which was streaming through the high windows, falling across the parquet floor. It was still; there was not a soul in the adjoining rooms. Pyotr Alexandrovitch was not at home, while Alexandra Mikhailovna was lying ill in bed. I was actually crying and, opening the second part of the book, I flicked aimlessly through the pages, trying to discover some meaning in the disconnected phrases that flitted before my eyes. I was trying my fortune, as people do, by opening a book at random. There are moments when all the intellectual and spiritual faculties, painfully overstrained, seem suddenly to blaze with the bright flame of consciousness. At these times the troubled soul, languishing with a presentiment, a foretaste of the future, has something akin to a prophetic vision. And the whole being longs to live, it cries out for life, and the heart, alight with blind, desperate hope, will invoke the future, with all its mystery and incertitude, its storms and tempests, if only it will bring life. This was one such moment.

I remember closing the book and opening it again at random to tell my future. But when I opened it I saw a sheet of paper folded in four and covered with handwriting. The paper had become so flat and dry that it must have slipped between the pages of the book years ago and then been forgotten. With great curiosity, I examined my discovery: it was not addressed to anyone, and was signed with the initials 'S.O.' My interest was redoubled. I unfolded the paper, which was stuck together and had discoloured the page of the book in the course of time. The folds in the paper were worn and cracked, and it was obvious that at one time it must have been read and reread, before it was preserved as something precious. The ink was faded and bluish; this letter had been written many years before. Several words that leapt up to my eye made my heart race in expectation. Confused, I turned the letter over in my hands, as if I had some reason to postpone the moment of reading it. I happened to hold it up to the light. Yes! Tears had fallen on some of the lines, drying and staining the paper; here and there whole words were erased by teardrops. Whose tears were they? At last, faint with expectation, I read half of the first page. I gasped in astonishment. Then I locked the bookcase, returned the key to its place, hid the letter under my shawl and ran to my room. I locked the door and read it from beginning to end. My heart pounded so much that the words and letters flitted and danced before my eyes. It was some time before I could make anything out at all. The letter was a revelation, the unlocking of a secret; it struck me like a flash of lightning, because I knew the person to whom it was written. I knew that I had done wrong to read the letter, but the excitement was overwhelming! It was addressed to Alexandra Mikhailovna. I shall quote it here. The realization of what it contained dawned on me slowly, and for a long time afterwards I was haunted by conjectures and painful surmises. From that moment my life was shattered. My heart was agitated and disturbed for a very long time, in fact right up to the present, because the letter aroused so much within me. I had, truly, guessed the future.

It was a farewell letter, one of terrible finality. As I read it I felt my heart contracting painfully, as though I had myself lost everything, as though it had all been taken from me for ever, even my dreams and my hopes, as though nothing more was left to me than a futile existence. Who was he, the writer of the letter? What was her life like afterwards? There were so many allusions in the letter, so many facts, that there could be no mistake; and yet at the same time there were so many riddles that one became lost in conjecture. But I was hardly mistaken: the whole tone of the letter, with all its implications, revealed the nature of the relationship through which two hearts had been broken. The feelings, the writer's thoughts, were laid bare; they were so intense and, as I have already said, they implied so much. Here is the letter; I reproduce it word for word.

You said you would never forget me. I believe it, and henceforth all my life rests in those words of yours. We must part, our hour has struck! I have known this for a long time, my gentle, my sorrowful beauty, but only now do I understand it. Through all our time, throughout all the time that you loved me, my heart has yearned and ached on account of our love, and, believe it or not, I feel relieved now. I knew long ago that it would be like this, that we were destined to this from the beginning! It is fate! Let me tell you, Alexandra Mikhailovna, we are not EQUALS; I have always felt that, always! I was not worthy of you and I alone should suffer the penalty for my lost happiness. Tell me, what was I before I met you? Goodness, two years have passed, and I seem to have been unconscious of it until now; to this day I cannot grasp that YOU have loved ME. I do not understand how it all happened, how it began. Do you remember what I was compared to you? Was I worthy of you? In what did I excel, in what way was I remarkable? Until I knew you, I was coarse and common, my expression sullen and dejected. I had no desire for any other sort of life – I never thought about it, I never looked for it or even wanted to look for it. Everything in me was somehow crushed, and nothing in the world seemed more important to me than my daily work. My only concern was the morrow, and I was indifferent to that too. In the past – long, long ago – I had a dream of something like this and, like a fool, I gave way to my day-dreaming. But a very long time has passed since then; I had taken to living in solitude, calmly and drearily, and I actually could not feel the cold that froze my heart; and it withered. I believed that the sun would not shine again, and resolved that it would be so; I believed it and did not complain of anything, because I knew it was incontrovertible. When you crossed my path I dared not raise my eyes to yours; I was a servant before you. There was no tremor or pain in my heart when I was near you; it told me nothing, it was unmoved. My soul failed to recognize yours although it found new light beside its beautiful sister soul. I know that, I felt it dimly. That I *was* able to feel, since the light of God's day shines on the lowest blade of grass and warms and cherishes it, even though it grows beside a lovely flower. When I found out – do you remember? – after that evening, after those words which shook me to the depth of my soul, I was stunned, shattered, brimming over and – do you know this? – I was so overwhelmed, and had so little faith in myself, that I failed to understand you! I have never told you this. You know nothing of it. I was not the same in the past as I was when you found me. If I could have spoken and had dared to speak I would have confessed everything to you a long time ago. But I kept silent, and I am telling you all now so that you may know the man you are leaving. Do you know how I understood you at first? Passion consumed me like fire, flowing like poison through my blood, stirring up my thoughts and feelings. It was as if I was intoxicated, possessed, and I responded to your pure, compassionate love not as your equal, not as one worthy of that love, but senselessly and heartlessly. I did not recognize what you were. I responded to you as to one who in my eyes had LOWERED HERSELF TO MY LEVEL, not one who wanted to raise me to hers. Do you know of what I suspected you, what is meant by those words 'LOWERED TO MY LEVEL'? But no, I will not insult you with my confession; only one thing I will tell you: you were bitterly mistaken in me! Never, never could I have risen to your level. I could only contemplate you in boundless love, without ever approaching you. My passion, aroused by you, was not love; I was afraid of love; I dared not love you; love implies reciprocity, equality, and I was not worthy of them . . . I do not know how it was with me! Ah! How can I tell you this, how can I make myself understood? . . . I did not believe it at first . . . Oh! Do you remember when my first excitement had subsided, when I could see things more clearly, when nothing was left but pure feeling cleansed of all that was gross? My first emotion was one of surprise, confusion, fright and – do you remember? – all at once I fell sobbing at your feet. Do you remember how, confused and frightened, you kept asking, with tears in your eyes: what was I feeling? I said nothing, I could not answer you, but my heart was torn apart; my happiness weighed me down, it was unbearable, and my sobs seemed to whisper inside me: 'Why is this happening? How have I deserved it? What have I done to be granted such bliss? My sister, my sister!' Oh! How many times – you never knew it – how many times I secretly kissed your dress, secretly because I knew I was not worthy of you; and I could hardly breathe at such times; my heart beat slowly, as if about to stop once and for all. When I took your hand I was pale and trembling all over; you confounded me with the purity of your soul. Ah, I cannot tell you all that has been accumulating in my heart, longing to be expressed! Did you realize how your constant and compassionate tenderness was a burden and torture to me? When you kissed me (it happened once and I will never forget it), there was a mist before my eyes and my heart stood still. Why did I not die at your feet in that moment? I am using the familiar form with you for the first time, although you asked me to do so a long time ago. Can you understand what it is I am trying to say? I want to tell you EVERYTHING, and I will tell you this: yes, you loved me very much, you loved me as a sister loves a brother; you loved me as your own creation, because it was you who resurrected my heart; you awakened my slumbering mind and filled my heart with sweet hope. But I could not and dared not call you my sister, because I could not be your brother; because we were not equal; because you are mistaken in me!

But, you see, I am writing all this while about myself; even now, at this fearful moment of misery, I can only think of myself, although I am sure you are worrying about me. Oh, do not worry, dear one! If you only knew how humiliated I am in my own eyes! Everything has come out – oh, what a scandal there has been! You will be an outcast on account of me. You will be scorned and jeered at because I am so low in their eyes! Oh, it's all my fault for being unworthy of you! If only I was somebody, if only I was of some worth in their eyes and could inspire them with more respect, then they might have forgiven you! But I am low, I am insignificant, I am absurd, and nothing is worse than being absurd. WHO are they to make a fuss? Because of THEM I have lost heart; I have always been weak. Do you know the state I am in now? I am laughing at myself, and it seems to me that they are right, because I am absurd and hateful even to myself. That is what I feel; I hate even my face, my figure, all my habits, all my ignoble ways. I have always hated them. Oh, forgive me my crude despair! It is you who taught me to tell everything. I have been your ruin; I have brought anger and contempt upon you because I was beneath you.

And it is this thought that troubles me, that hammers incessantly through my head and poisons my wounded heart: it still seems to me that you loved the man you thought you found in me, that you were deceived by me. That is what hurts, that is what tortures me and will torment me to death, if I do not lose my mind.

Farewell, farewell! Now, when everything is discovered; when the hue and cry begin, and the gossips (for I have heard them); when I have been humiliated, degraded in my own mind, made to feel ashamed of myself, ashamed for your choice; when I have cursed myself – now I must run away and disappear for your sake. They demand it, so you will never see me again, *never*! It must be so, it is fated! I was given too much; fortune erred and now she must correct the mistake and take everything back. We came together, we got to know each other and now we must part until we meet again. When will that be? Where will it be? Oh, tell me, darling, where shall we meet again? Where shall I find you? How shall I know you, and will you know me then? My whole soul is full of you. Oh, why is it, why should this happen to us? Why are we parting? Teach me, I do not understand. Teach me how to wrench my life in two, how to tear my heart out of my breast, how to live without it. Ah, to think that I shall never see you again, never, never! . . .

My God! What a commotion they have raised. I am terrified for you now! I have only just met your husband; we are both unworthy of him, though neither of us has sinned against him. He knows everything; he sees us and understands all. It was crystal clear to him from the start. He has stood up for you heroically; he will save you; he will defend you against their gossip, against the uproar; he has boundless respect and love for you. He is your saviour, while I ran away! I rushed to him, I wanted to kiss his hand. He told me to leave without delay. It is settled! They say that he has quarrelled with all of them on your account; they are all against you! They reproach him for indulgence and weakness! My God! What do they not say about you? They do not know, THEY CANNOT UNDERSTAND, THEY ARE INCAPABLE OF IT. My poor darling, please forgive them as I am forgiving them. They have taken more from me than from you!

I am beside myself, I do not know what I am writing. What did I say to you yesterday when we parted? You see, I have forgotten everything. I was distracted and you were crying . . . Forgive me for those tears, I am so weak and cowardly!

There was another thing I wanted to say to you . . . Oh, if only my tears could fall on your hands again as they now fall on this letter! To be at your feet once more! If THEY only knew how noble your feelings are! But they are blind; their hearts are proud and arrogant; they do not see it and will never see it. Their eyes see NOTHING! They will not believe that you are innocent, even according to their own standards – not even if everything on this earth testified to it. As if they could understand this! How can *they* throw stones at you? Whose hand will throw the first? Oh, they have no qualms, they will cast a thousand stones. They will fling them boldly, for they know how to do it. They will throw them at once and then say they are without sin, and will take the sin on themselves. If only it were possible to tell them every-thing, quite openly and clearly so that they might see, hear, understand and believe! . . . But no, they are not that wicked . . . In despair now, I am perhaps unfair to them. Nor do I wish to frighten you – do not be afraid of them, my darling. They will understand you; after all one of them already understands you; take heart: he is your husband.

Farewell, farewell! I WILL NOT THANK YOU.
Farewell for ever! S.O.

I was so confused that it took me a while to realize what was happening to me. I was shocked and frightened. In the midst of a simple life of dreams, on which I had lived for three years, reality had caught me by surprise. I was frightened to think that I was holding a great mystery in my hands, and that this mystery was now linked with my whole existence . . . But how? I did not know the answer to that. At the time I felt as if a new life were beginning for me. I had become an involuntary participant in the lives and personal relations of those who up until that time had comprised my whole world, and I was now becoming afraid for myself. How should I, an outsider, enter uninvited into this life? What could I bring to them? How would these fetters, that had so suddenly fastened me to another's secret, be loosened? Who could tell, perhaps my new role would be distressing both to me and to others. Yet I could not remain silent, I could not refuse to accept this role and seal up what I knew in my heart for ever. What might come of it? What ought I to do? And what, after all, had I discovered? Thousands of still vague and confused questions arose in my mind and already weighed heavily on my heart. I felt lost.

Later, I remember, came another phase, when my impressions were quite strange and different from anything I had ever experienced before; I felt as if something had been resolved within me, and that the old sadness had left my heart and something new was taking its place – something over which I still knew not whether to grieve or rejoice. I felt like a person who is leaving for good a home and a hitherto peaceful and unruffled life, setting out on some long and unknown journey, who looks around for the last time, thoughtfully bidding farewell to the past, feeling sick at heart and full of misgivings about the harsh and hostile future that perhaps is waiting on the road.

Eventually I broke into convulsions of sobbing and relieved

my heart with hysterical tears. I had to see someone, to hear someone, to hold someone tight. I could no longer remain by myself; I rushed to Alexandra Mikhailovna and spent the whole evening with her. We were alone. I asked her not to play the piano, and although she wanted me to I refused to sing. I could not concentrate on anything; everything seemed impossibly difficult. I believe we were both crying. I remember her becoming quite alarmed about me and trying to persuade me to calm myself and not be so distressed. She watched me in dismay, insisting that I was still not looking after myself properly. When at last I left her, I was worn out and preoccupied. I went to bed in a feverish state, verging on delirium.

Several days passed before I regained my self-possession and was able to consider my position more clearly. At this time Alexandra Mikhailovna and I were both living in complete solitude and Pyotr Alexandrovitch was not at home. He had gone to Moscow on business and was away for three weeks. Although this was not a long time, Alexandra Mikhailovna fell into a state of utter despondency. There were times when she was more composed, but she kept herself shut up in her room and found my presence irritating. Besides, I myself was seeking isolation. My mind was constantly turning, and I was under severe nervous strain. I was more or less in a daze and sometimes, for long hours, I would be fraught with harassing disconnected thoughts. Then I would imagine that someone was secretly mocking me; it was as though there was something inside me that confused and poisoned my mind. I could find no escape from the tormenting images that rose before me at every moment, giving me no peace. I envisaged long and hopeless suffering, martyrdom, sacrifice endured meekly, abjectly and fruitlessly. It seemed to me that the one for whom the sacrifice was made scorned and derided it. I saw a criminal pardoning the sins of the righteous, and my heart was torn. At the same time I longed to free myself of suspicion; I cursed and hated myself because all my convictions were more like presentiments, and because I could not justify my impressions to myself.

I went through all the phrases in my mind: those last, terrible cries of farewell. I pictured to myself that man who was

BENEATH HER; I tried to fathom the agonizing significance of those words. I was deeply moved by the note of despair in the farewell: 'I am absurd ... ashamed for your choice ...' What did it mean? Who were they? Why were they grieving? What was tormenting them? What had they lost? Composing myself with an effort, I tensely reread the letter which was so full of despair, heartbroken though its meaning was still obscure and incomprehensible to me. But the letter fell from my hands and my heart was increasingly strained with emotion ... All this had somehow to be resolved, but I could see no way out; I lived in dread!

I was virtually ill when the carriage rumbled into the court-yard one day, bringing Pyotr Alexandrovitch, who had returned from Moscow. Alexandra Mikhailovna flew to meet her husband with a cry of joy, but I stood rooted to the spot. I remember that I was surprised at my sudden emotion. I could not control myself and rushed to my room. I did not understand why I suddenly felt so alarmed, but it frightened me. A quarter of an hour later I was summoned and given a letter from Prince X. In the drawing-room I met a stranger whom Pyotr Alexandrovitch had brought from Moscow; from what I gathered he was to stay with us for some time. He was the agent of Prince X. and was here in Petersburg to take care of certain important family matters which had long been supervised by Pyotr Alexandrovitch. He handed me the letter from the Prince and told me that the young Princess had also wished to write, and had even assured him right up until the last moment that the letter would be ready, but in the end he had left empty-handed. She had begged him to tell me that there was absolutely no use in her writing, since it was impossible to express anything in a letter, that she had spoilt at least five sheets of notepaper before tearing them up, and that we would have to make friends all over again before we could write to each other. Afterwards she instructed him to assure me that we would meet again before long. In answer to my eager questions, the unknown gentleman said that an early meeting was quite certain, as the whole family would be visiting Petersburg before long. I was over-whelmed with joy at this news; I rushed to my room, locked myself in and dissolved into tears as I opened the Prince's letter. In it he promised that I would soon see both him and Katya again and he congratulated me, with deep feeling, on my talent; finally he gave me his blessing and best wishes for the future, which he promised to provide for. I wept as I read this letter, but with those tears of joy was mixed such an insufferable sadness that I remember being alarmed at myself, for I did not know what was happening to me.

Several days passed. In the room next to mine, which had previously been the office of Pyotr Alexandrovitch's secretary, the newcomer now worked every morning and frequently through the evening up until midnight. Often this gentleman and Pyotr Alexandrovitch shut themselves in the latter's study and worked together. One day Alexandra Mikhailovna told me to go into her husband's study and ask him whether he would come and have tea with us. Finding no one in the study, and expecting Pyotr Alexandrovitch to come back shortly, I waited for him. His portrait was hanging on the wall. I remember that I shuddered as I looked at the portrait, and with an excitement I could not myself understand I began scrutinizing it intently. It was hung rather high, and as it was getting dark in the room I pushed a chair up and stood on it in order to see better. I wanted to find something which might provide the solution to my doubts. What struck me first of all was the eyes in the portrait. Immediately it occurred to me that I had never seen the eyes of this man before; he always kept them hidden behind spectacles.

Even in my childhood, from some strange, unaccountable prejudice, I had disliked the way he looked at people, but now that prejudice seemed to be justified. My imagination was roused. It suddenly seemed to me as though the eyes of the portrait were, in confusion, turning away from my searching, questioning gaze, that they were trying to avoid it, and that there was a duplicity in those eyes; it appeared that I had been right, and I cannot explain the secret joy that stirred in me at having guessed correctly. I uttered a faint cry and at that moment I heard a rustle behind me. I looked round and saw Pyotr Alexandrovitch standing before me, staring at me. I thought I saw him redden. I blushed and jumped down from the chair.

'What are you doing here?' he asked in a stern voice. 'Why are you here?'

I did not know what to answer. Recovering myself a little, I gave him Alexandra Mikhailovna's message. I do not know what answer he gave and I do not remember how I escaped from the room, but when I reached Alexandra Mikhailovna I had complete forgotten the answer for which she was waiting. I said, at a guess, that he was coming.

'But what's the matter with you, Netochka?' she asked. 'You are so flushed. Look at yourself! What's the matter with you?'

'I don't know ... I was hurrying –' I began to answer.

'What did Pyotr Alexandrovitch say to you?' she interrupted, troubled.

I did not answer. At that moment Pyotr Alexandrovitch's footsteps were heard and I instantly walked out of the room. I waited for two hours in great anxiety. At last I was summoned to Alexandra Mikhailovna. I found her silent and preoccupied. As I went into the room she cast a rapid, searching glance at me and then at once lowered her eyes. She seemed disconcerted. I realized that she was in a bad mood; she spoke little, did not look at me at all and, in reply to B.'s inquiries, said that she had a headache. Pyotr Alexandrovitch was more talkative than usual, but he spoke only to B.

Alexandra Mikhailovna walked absentmindedly over to the piano.

'Sing something,' said B., turning to me.

'Yes, Annetta, sing your new aria,' added Alexandra Mikhailovna, as if pleased by the suggestion. I glanced at her. She was looking at me in anxious expectation.

But I could not control myself. Instead of going to the piano and singing, I was overcome with uncertainty, and in my embarrassment I could not think of a way to excuse myself. In the end my annoyance got the upper hand, and I refused outright.

'Why don't you want to sing?' said Alexandra Mikhailovna, throwing a lengthy, significant glance at me and a fleeting one at her husband.

Those two glances provoked me. I got up from the table in a state of complete confusion. No longer trying to conceal it, but shaking with a feeling of impatience and annoyance, I hotly repeated that I did not want to, I could not, that I was unwell. As I said this I looked them each in the eye. God knows how I longed at that moment to be in my own room and to hide myself from all of them.

B. was surprised; Alexandra Mikhailovna was visibly upset, and did not say a word. But Pyotr Alexandrovitch sprang from his chair and said that he had forgotten some work. He was evidently annoyed at having lost valuable time and hurried out of the room, saying that he might look in later, but in case he did not he shook hands with B. by way of goodbye.

'What's the matter with you?' asked B. 'You look really ill.'

'Yes, I'm unwell, very unwell,' I answered impatiently.

'Indeed you are very pale, and just a short time ago you were so flushed,' remarked Alexandra Mikhailovna abruptly.

'Do stop!' I said, going straight up to her and looking her in the face. The poor thing could not look me in the eyes – she dropped hers as if guilty, and a faint flush suffused her pale cheeks. I took her hand and kissed it. Alexandra Mikhailovna looked at me with a show of naïve joy.

'Excuse me for being such a bad, ill-tempered child today,' I said to her with sincerity, 'but really I am ill. Let me go, and don't be angry.'

'We are all children,' she said with a meek smile. 'And indeed I'm a child too, and worse, much worse than you,' she added in my ear. 'Good night; get better. Only, for God's sake, don't be cross with me.'

'Why should I?' I asked, struck by this naïve confession.

'Why should you?' she echoed, terribly confused and even frightening herself. 'Why? Well, you see what I'm like, Net-ochka. What did I say to you? Good night! You're cleverer than I . . . and I'm worse than a child.'

'Come, that's enough,' I answered, much moved, and not knowing what to say to her. I kissed her once more and went hurriedly out of the room.

I felt horribly troubled and sad. Besides this, I was angry with myself, feeling that I was too careless and did not know how to behave. I was mortified and at the point of tears. I went to bed in a state of deep depression. When I woke up in the morning my first thought was that the whole previous evening had been just a fantasy, an illusion which we had created for one another, exaggerating the importance of what we felt in our anxiety; all this was due to inexperience and to our habit of ignoring the outward aspect of things. I felt that the letter was to blame for it all, that it was upsetting me too much, and that my imagination was overwrought, and I resolved that in the future I had better not think about anything. Once I had settled all my troubles with such exceptional ease and convinced myself that I could carry out my resolve with equal ease, I felt calmer and set off for my singing lesson in quite a cheerful mood. The morning air completely cleared away my headache. I was very fond of morning walks to my lessons. It was so pleasant going through the town, which by nine o'clock was already full of life and busily starting its daily round. We usually passed through the liveliest and busiest streets. It pleased me that my artistic life was beginning in these surroundings. I enjoyed the contrast between the petty everyday life, the trivial but vital cares, and the art which awaited me two steps away from this life, on the third storey of a huge house crowded from top to bottom with inhabitants who, it seemed to me, had nothing whatsoever to do with art. These busy, frustrated-looking passers-by, among whom I went with my music book under my arm; old Natalya, who accompanied me and always, unconsciously, made me wonder what she was thinking about; my teacher – a queer fellow, half-Italian, half-French – who was at times genuinely enthusiastic but more often pedantic and mean; all this entertained me and made me laugh and wonder. Moreover, I loved music with passionate though diffident hope; I built castles in the air, pictured the most marvellous future and often, as I returned home, was quite transported by my own fantasies. In fact, for those hours, I was almost happy. I had one such moment that day, at ten o'clock when I was on my way home from my lesson. I had forgotten everything, and I remember that I was happily dreaming. But, all at once, as I was going upstairs, I started as though I had been scalded. Above me I heard the voice of Pyotr Alexandrovitch, who at that moment was coming downstairs. The unpleasant feeling that came over me was so intense, the recollection of the previous day's incident filled me with so much displeasure, that I could not conceal my alarm. I made a slight bow to him, but my face probably gave me away at that moment, for he stopped short and faced me in surprise. Seeing his movements, I flushed crimson and hurried upstairs; he muttered something after me and went on his way. I was upset and wanted to cry, unable to understand what had happened. I was not myself all morning and did not know what action to take to make an end of it, to be rid of it all as quickly as possible. A thousand times I vowed to myself to be more sensible, and a thousand times I was overwhelmed with the fear of what I had to do. I felt that I hated Alexandra Mikhailovna's husband and yet, at the same time, I was in despair over my own behaviour. The ceaseless agitation was making me ill, and I was losing control. I felt annoyed with everyone; sat in my room all morning and did not even go to see Alexandra Mikhailovna. She came to me. She almost cried out when she caught sight of me. I was so pale that I frightened myself when I looked in the mirror. Alexandra Mikhailovna spent a whole hour with me, tending to me as if I were a little child.

But her concern and kindness made me more miserable. It was so painful to look at her that I finally asked her to leave me alone. She went away, greatly troubled about me. At last my misery found a vent in tears and hysteria. Towards evening I felt better ...

Better, because I made up my mind to go to her. I decided to fall at her feet, to give her the letter she had lost, and to confess everything: all the agonies I had endured, all my doubts; to embrace her with the infinite love that glowed in my heart for her, my martyr; to tell her that I was her child, her friend, that my heart was open to her, that she must look into it and see the ardent, unshakeable feelings for her reflected there. My God! I felt as though I would be the last person to whom she could open her heart, but it seemed perhaps that would make salvation more certain and the effect of my words more powerful ... Albeit vaguely and obscurely, I did understand her sufferings, and my heart seethed with indignation at the thought that she could possibly bow before me, before my judgement ... Poor darling, my poor darling, as if *you* were a sinner! That is what I would say to her as I wept at her feet. My sense of justice was revolted; I was incensed. What I would have happened I do not know, but just as soon as I recovered myself, an unforeseen occurrence prevented my first move and saved us both from ruin. I was aghast. Would her tortured heart have risen to hope again? I would have killed her if I had told her.

This is what happened. I was on my way to her study and just two rooms away from it, when Pyotr Alexandrovitch came in by a side-door and, not noticing me, went on ahead of me. He, too, was going to see her. I stood stock-still; he was the last person I wanted to meet at such a moment. I wanted to turn back, but my curiosity rooted me to the spot.

He stood for a minute before the looking-glass, smoothed his hair, and, to my immense astonishment, I suddenly heard him humming some kind of tune. Instantly an obscure, distant memory belonging to my childhood rose in my mind. To clarify the strange sensation I felt at that moment, I shall describe the memory. It was of an incident that had made a profound impression upon me in the first year of my life in that house, although its significance was only now becoming clear, for only now, only at this moment, did I realize the origin of the inexplicable antipathy I felt for this man! I have already mentioned that, even in those days, I always felt ill at ease with him. I have already described the depressing effect on me of his frowning, nervous air, and the expression on his face, which was so frequently melancholy and despondent; I have already told how unhappy I was after the hours we spent together at Alexandra Mikhailovna's tea-table and what terrible misery rent my heart on the two or three occasions when it was my misfortune to witness those gloomy, oppressive scenes. It happened that I had come upon him then just as I did now – in the same room, at the same time, when we were both on our way to see Alexandra Mikhailovna. I had been overwhelmed with purely childish shyness at meeting him alone and hid in a corner as if I had done something wrong, praying that he would not notice me. Then, just as now, he had stopped before the looking-glass, and I shuddered with a vague, unchildlike feeling. It seemed to me as if he were making up his face. Anyway, I had seen him smiling before he approached the looking-glass, then laughing. I had never seen him laugh, for (I remember it was this that struck me most of all) he never did so in the presence of Alexandra Mikhailovna. But as soon as he had looked in the glass his face had changed completely. The smile on his lips had disappeared as if at a word of command and had been replaced by a look of bitterness which appeared to spring from his heart spontaneously, involuntarily; a feeling which it had seemed beyond his power to disguise, in spite of tremendous effort, and which like a spasm of pain had distorted his mouth and creased his brow. His eyes had been deeply concealed behind his spectacles; in brief, he had seemed, at a given signal, to be changed into a different man. I remember that, as a little child, I had shuddered with the fear and dread of understanding what I had seen, and from then onwards an uneasy, disagreeable impression was locked in my heart for ever. After looking at himself for a minute in the glass he had lowered his head and hunched his shoulders, which was his normal posture when in the presence of his wife, and then he had tiptoed to her room. This was the memory that came back to me.

On that occasion, as now, he had thought he was alone when he stopped before the mirror. And now, as before, I felt antagonism and unpleasantness when I found myself on my own with him. But when I heard this tune (a tune from him, of whom one would never have expected such a thing), I was so taken aback that I stood rooted to the spot. I was reminded of a similar moment in my childhood, and I cannot describe the bitter feeling which thumped in my heart. All my nerves began to quiver, and my unfortunate reaction to this tune was to break into peals of laughter, so that the poor man cried out, stepping back a couple of paces from the mirror and turning deadly pale. He looked at me as if he had been shamefully caught in the act, beside himself with alarm, astonishment and fury. But his expression had a disastrous effect on me, and I laughed uncontrollably and nervously into his face as I walked past him into Alexandra Mikhailovna's room. I knew that he was standing behind the curtains, that he was perhaps hesitating over whether to come in or not, that he was paralysed with rage and cowardice and, in my nervous, defiant impatience, I wanted to see what he would do. I was quite sure that he would not come in, and I was right. It was half an hour before he entered. Alexandra Mikhailovna looked at me for a long time in the utmost perplexity, but her inquiries as to what was the matter with me were in vain. I could not tell her; I was gasping for breath. At last she realized that I was in hysterics and anxiously tended to me. When I had recovered I took her hands and began kissing them. Only then did I see what was happening, and only then did the thought occur to me that I should have been the death of her had it not been for that moment's encounter with her husband. I looked at her as though she had risen from the dead.

Pyotr Alexandrovitch walked in. I gave him a furtive glance. His appearance gave the impression that nothing had happened between us; that is, he was as austere and gloomy as always. But, from his pale face and the faintly twitching corners of his mouth, I guessed that he could hardly conceal his agitation. He greeted Alexandra Mikhailovna coldly and sat down at his place without a word. His hand trembled as he took his cup of tea. I expected some outburst and was overcome by an incalculable terror. I would have liked to go, but I could not bring myself to leave Alexandra Mikhailovna, whose mood had also changed when she saw her husband. She too had a foreboding of trouble. What I was anticipating so fearfully happened at last.

In the middle of a deep silence I lifted my eyes and met Pyotr Alexandrovitch's spectacles turned directly towards me. It was so unexpected that I started, almost cried out, and then lowered my eyes. Alexandra Mikhailovna noticed my agitation.

'What's the matter with you? Why are you blushing?' resounded Pyotr Alexandrovitch's harsh voice.

I said nothing; my heart was throbbing and I could not answer a word.

'What's she blushing at? Why's she always blushing?' he asked, addressing Alexandra Mikhailovna and pointing rudely at me.

I could hardly breathe for indignation. I cast a beseeching glance at Alexandra Mikhailovna. She understood me. Her pale cheeks flushed.

'Annetta,' she said to me in a firm voice, which I would never have expected from her, 'go to your room. I'll come to you in a minute, and we'll spend the evening together –'

'I asked you a question! Did you hear me or not?' Pyotr Alexandrovitch interrupted, raising his voice still higher, and seeming not to hear what his wife had said. 'Why do you blush when you meet me? Answer!'

'Because you make her blush as you do me,' said Alexandra Mikhailovna in an agitated, broken voice. I looked at her in amazement. The unexpected passion of her remark baffled me for a moment.

'*I* make you blush, *I*?' answered Pyotr Alexandrovitch, apparently in a fury. '*You* have blushed for *me*? Do you mean to tell me I can make *you* blush for *me*? It's for *me* to blush, not for you, don't you think?'

This phrase, uttered with such callous, caustic sarcasm, was so clear to me that I cried out in horror and rushed to Alexandra Mikhailovna. Surprise, pain, reproach and fear were all depicted on her face, which began to turn a deathly pale. Clasping my hands with a look of entreaty, I glanced at Pyotr Alexandrovitch. He seemed to realize that he had gone too far, but the fury that had driven those words out had not yet subsided. However, when he noticed my silent plea, he was confused. My gesture clearly betrayed that I knew what had hitherto been a secret between them, and that I fully understood the meaning of his words.

'Annetta, go to your room,' repeated Alexandra Mikhailovna in a quiet but firm voice, as she stood up. 'I want to speak to Pyotr Alexandrovitch ...' She was calm on the surface, but that calm frightened me more than any agitation would have done. I stood quite still, behaving as if I had not heard what she said ... I strained every nerve to read in her face what was going on in her heart at that moment. It seemed to me that she had understood neither my gesture nor my exclamation.

'See what you have done, miss!' said Pyotr Alexandrovitch, taking my hand and pointing to his wife.

My goodness! I have never seen such despair as I saw now on that stricken, deathly-looking face. I glanced back again as he led me out of the room. I took one last look at them. Alexandra Mikhailovna was standing with her elbows on the mantelpiece, holding her head tightly between both hands. Her whole attitude expressed unbearable torture. I seized Pyotr Alexandrovitch's hand and squeezed it warmly.

'For God's sake, for God's sake!' I cried in a broken voice. 'Spare her!'

'Don't be afraid, don't be afraid,' he said, looking at me strangely. 'It's nothing, it's nerves. Go on, run along.'

In my room, I threw myself on the sofa and hid my face in my hands. For three whole hours I remained in that position, and I passed through perfect hell during those hours. At last I could bear it no longer and sent to inquire whether I could go to Alexandra Mikhailovna. Madame Léotard brought me the answer. Pyotr Alexandrovitch said that the attack had passed and there was nothing to be alarmed about, but that she needed peace and quiet. I did not go to bed until three in the morning, but walked up and down the room thinking. My position was more perplexing than ever, but I somehow felt calmer, perhaps because I felt that I was more to blame than anyone. I went to bed impatient for the following day.

But the next day, to my surprise and sorrow, I noticed an inexplicable coldness in Alexandra Mikhailovna. At first I fancied that it was painful to her pure and noble heart to be with me after the scene the day before with her husband, of which I had unfortunately been a witness. I knew that the childlike creature was capable of blushing and begging my forgiveness for that unfortunate episode, which she may have felt offended me, but I soon noticed a very different sort of anxiety and annoyance, which was expressed very awkwardly. At times she answered me in a cold, dry tone, while at other times there seemed to be some peculiar pointedness in what she said. Then she would become very tender with me, as if repenting the harshness which she could not feel in her heart, and there was a note of self-reproach in her affectionate and gentle words. At last I asked her directly what was the matter and whether she had anything to say to me. She was a little taken aback at my sudden question but, raising her large, clear eyes and looking at me with a sweet smile, she said: 'It's nothing, Netochka. But when you asked me so abruptly you confused me. That was only because you were so abrupt . . . I assure you. But listen . . . tell me the truth, my child: have you got anything on your mind which might have made you confused at suddenly being questioned in that way?'

'No,' I answered, looking into her clear eyes.

'Well, that's a good thing! You don't know, my dear, how grateful I am to you for that good answer. Not that I could suspect you of anything bad – no, never. I could not forgive myself such a thought. But listen . . . I took you as a child, and now you are seventeen. You've seen for yourself that I'm ill, that I'm like a child that needs to be looked after. I cannot be a proper mother to you, although there's more than enough love in my heart for it. If I am tormented with worry, as I am now, it is, of course, not your fault, but mine. Forgive me for the question and for having perhaps failed, in spite of myself, to keep all the promises I made to you and my father when I took you into my house. I've been very worried about it for some time.'

I kissed her and burst into tears.

'Oh, thank you . . . thank you for everything,' I said, bathing her hands with my tears. 'Don't talk to me in that way, don't break my heart. You've been more than a mother to me. May God bless you and the Prince for all you have done for me, a poor abandoned child.'

'Hush, Netochka, hush! Hug me instead; that's right, hold me tight! Do you know, I believe – I don't know why – that this is the last time you will embrace me.'

'No, no,' I said, sobbing like a child. 'No, that cannot be. You'll be happy . . . You have many days ahead of you, Believe me, we'll be happy.'

'Thank you, thank you for loving me so much. I have not many friends near to me now; they have all deserted me!'

'Who has deserted you? Who?'

'There used to be other people, Netochka, you don't know. They have all left me. They have all faded away as if they were ghosts. And I have been waiting for them, waiting for them all my life. God be with them. Look, Netochka, you see it is late autumn, soon the snow will be here. With the first snow I shall die, but I do not regret it. Farewell.'

Her face was thin and pale; an ominous patch of red glowed on each cheek; her lips quivered and were parched with fever.

She went up to the piano and struck a few chords; a string snapped and with a clang died away in a long discordant note . . .

'Do you hear, Netochka, do you hear?' she said, pointing to the piano as if it had suddenly inspired her. 'That string was strained to breaking-point, it could bear it no more and has perished. Do you hear how plaintively the sound dies away?' She spoke with difficulty. Mute spiritual anguish was reflected in her face, and her eyes were filled with tears.

'Come now, Netochka, enough of that, my dear. Fetch the children.'

I brought them in. She seemed to relax as she watched them. She sent them away an hour later.

'You won't forsake them when I die, will you, Netochka?' she whispered, as though afraid someone might overhear us.

'Stop, I can't bear it!' was all I could say in reply.

'But I'm only joking,' she said after a moment's silence, and smiled. 'You didn't believe me, did you? Sometimes I talk utter nonsense. I'm like a child now, you must forgive me everything.'

Then she looked at me timidly, as if afraid of saying something. I waited.

'Mind you don't upset him,' she said at last, lowering her eyes and flushing a little. I could hardly hear her, she spoke so softly.

'Who?' I asked in surprise.

'My husband. You might perhaps tell him everything I said.'

'What for? . . . What for?' I said, more and more startled.

'Well, perhaps you wouldn't tell him, how can I say!' she answered, trying to glance slyly at me – though the same simple-hearted smile was on her lips and the colour was flowing into her face. 'Enough of that . . . I'm still joking, you know.' My heart started aching even more.

'But you will love them when I'm dead, won't you?' she asked gravely, adding with a somewhat mysterious air, 'You'll love them as if they were your own, won't you? Remember, I've always considered you as if *you* were my own and made no distinction between you and my children.'

'Yes, yes,' I answered, not knowing what I was saying and choking with tears and confusion.

Before I could withdraw it, I felt a burning kiss on my hand. I was left dumbfounded. What was the matter with her? What was she thinking? What had happened between them yesterday? These thoughts floated through my mind.

A minute later she began to complain that she was tired.

'I've been ill for a long time, but I didn't want to frighten you both,' she said. 'You both love me, don't you? . . . Goodbye, Netochka. Leave me now, but be sure to come back in the evening. You will, won't you?' I promised to do so, but I was glad to get away. I could not bear any more.

'Poor darling, poor darling! What kind of suspicions are you taking with you to the grave?' I exclaimed to myself, sobbing. 'What new trouble is poisoning and tormenting your heart, without your daring to talk about it? My God! This endless suffering, I understand it so well now! This life without a ray of hope . . . this timid love that asks for nothing! And even now, *now*, almost on her deathbed, with pain tearing her heart in two, she is afraid, like a criminal, of uttering the faintest murmur, the slightest complaint; as she imagines – invents – some new sorrow, she has already submitted to it, already resigned herself to it . . .'

Towards evening, in the twilight, I took advantage of the absence of Ovrov (the man who had come from Moscow) to go to the library and, unlocking a bookcase, I began rummaging through the books, looking for something light and frivolous to read aloud to Alexandra Mikhailovna. I wanted to distract her from her gloomy thoughts. For a long time I glanced absently through the books. It got darker, and my depression increased. Once again I found myself with that same book in my hands, open at the same page. Even now I could see the imprint of the letter which had never left my bosom since that day and which had disrupted my old existence. The secret in that letter had taken me into a world where there was so much that was cold, unknown, mysterious and hostile, even from a distance – and it was now closing in on me ... What would happen to me, I wondered ... the corner in which I felt so safe and secure would be empty! The pure, shining spirit that guarded my youth would leave me. What lay ahead? I remained lost in my thoughts of the past, now so dear to my heart, and at the same time I strove to see ahead into the vacuum which was threatening me ... I remember the moment as if I were reliving it now; it cut so sharply into my memory.

I was holding the letter and the open book in my hands, and my face was wet with tears. All at once I started with fright; I heard the sound of a familiar voice. At the same time I felt the letter being snatched out of my hands. I shrieked and looked around: Pyotr Alexandrovitch stood before me. He seized me by the arm and held me firmly. With his right hand he raised the letter to the light and tried to decipher the first lines ... I cried out, and would have faced death rather than give him the letter. From his triumphant smile I saw that he had succeeded in making out the content. I lost my head ...

A moment later, in a move of desperation, I snatched the letter from his hand, hardly knowing what I was doing. Everything happened so quickly that I did not have time to realize how I got hold of it again, but, seeing that he was about to snatch it back from me, I thrust it into the bodice of my dress and stepped back three or four paces.

We looked at one another for a minute in silence. I was still trembling with fear. He was pale; his lips were blue and quivering with rage. At last he broke the silence.

'Enough!' he said in a voice weak with emotion. 'You surely don't want me to resort to force. Give me back the letter of your own accord.'

Only at this point did I stop to think, and I found myself outraged. I was filled with resentment, shame and indignation at his coarse brutality. Warm tears streamed down my burning cheeks. I trembled all over with excitement and for some time I was unable to utter a word.

'Did you hear me?' he said, advancing a couple of paces in my direction.

'Leave me alone, leave me alone!' I cried, moving away from him. 'Your behaviour is contemptible and dishonourable. You're forgetting yourself! Let me go! . . .'

'What? What's the meaning of this? How dare you talk to me like that . . . Give it to me, I'm ordering you!' He took another step towards me but, glancing at me, saw such determination in my eyes that he hesitated.

'Very well,' he said drily, as though he had reached a decision but was hardly able to restrain himself. 'That will come in due course, but first . . .' He looked around. 'You . . . Who let you into the library? How is it that this bookcase is open? Where did you get the key?'

'I'm not going to answer you,' I said. 'I can't talk to you. Let me go . . . Let me go!' I stepped towards the door.

'Oh, no,' he said, holding me by the arm. 'You're not just going off like that.'

I tore my arm away from him without a word and again edged towards the door.

'Very well, then. But I really can't allow you to receive letters from your lovers in my house . . .'

I cried out frantically, and looked at him in horror . . .

'And so –'

'Stop!' I cried. 'How can you? How can you say that to me? My God! My God! . . .'

'What? What? Are you going to threaten me too?'

I gazed at him, pale and overwhelmed with despair. The scene between us had reached a degree of cruelty that was beyond my comprehension. My eyes begged him not to prolong it. I was ready to forgive the outrage if only he would stop. He looked at me intently and faltered visibly.

'Don't push me to the limit,' I whispered in horror.

'No, I must get to the bottom of this,' he said at last, after consideration. 'I confess that your look made me pause for a moment,' he added with a strange smile, 'but unfortunately the facts speak for themselves. I managed to read the first words of your letter. It's a love letter. You can't pretend otherwise. No! Dismiss that idea from your mind! And the fact that I could doubt it for a moment only proves that, to all your other excellent qualities, I must add a talent for lying, and I therefore repeat . . .'

. . . As he talked his face became more and more distorted with malice. He turned pale; his lips were drawn and twitching so that he could hardly articulate the last words. It was getting dark. I was standing defenceless, alone, facing a man who was not above insulting a woman. All the odds were against me too; I was tortured by shame, distracted, and unable to understand this man's fury. Without answering him I fled from the room racked with horror, and came to my senses only when I found myself standing outside the door to Alexandra Mikhailovna's sitting-room. I heard her footsteps and was about to enter the room when I stopped as if thunderstruck.

'What will happen to her?' was the thought that flashed through my mind. 'That letter! . . . No! Better anything in the world than that last blow to her . . .' and I made to rush back. But it was too late: he was standing beside me.

'Let's go anywhere you like, only not here, not here!' I whispered, clutching at his arm. 'Spare her! I'll go back to the library or . . . wherever you like! You'll kill her!'

'It's you who are killing her,' he said, pushing me away.

Every hope vanished. I felt that to bring the whole scene before Alexandra Mikhailovna was just what he wanted.

'For God's sake, don't,' I said, doing my utmost to hold him back. But at that moment the screen was drawn back and Alexandra Mikhailovna stood facing us. She looked at us in surprise. Her face was paler than ever, and she could barely stand on her feet. It had obviously cost her a great effort to come to the door when she heard our voices.

'Who's there? What are you talking about?' she asked, looking at us in complete amazement.

There was a prolonged silence; she turned as white as a sheet. I rushed over and, putting my arms around her, dragged her back to her sitting-room. Pyotr Alexandrovitch followed. I hid my face in her bosom and clung to her, numb with dread.

'What is it? What's the matter with you both?' asked Alexandra Mikhailovna for the second time.

'Ask *her*. Only yesterday you were defending her so fiercely,' said Pyotr Alexandrovitch, dropping heavily into an armchair. I continued to embrace her firmly.

'My God! What is this?' exclaimed Alexandra Mikhailovna in terrible dismay. 'You're so upset, and she's frightened and in tears. Annetta, tell me what's happened.'

'No, let me,' said Pyotr Alexandrovitch, coming over to us, taking me by the arm and pulling me away from Alexandra Mikhailovna. 'Stand there,' he said, placing me in the middle of the room. 'I wish to judge you in front of the woman who has been a mother to you. Please calm yourself and sit down,' he added to Alexandra Mikhailovna, seating her in an armchair. 'It grieves me that I can't spare you this distressing explanation, but now it's unavoidable.'

'Good heavens! What's coming?' said Alexandra Mikhailovna, in great distress, gazing alternately at me and at her husband. I wrung my hands, feeling that the fatal moment was at hand. I expected no mercy from him now.

'In short,' Pyotr Alexandrovitch went on, 'I want you to judge between us. You always (and I can't understand why, it's one of your whims), you always – yesterday for example – thought and said . . . but I don't know how to say it, I blush at the suggestion . . . In short, you defended her, you attacked me, you accused me of *undue* severity; you even hinted at *another* feeling, suggesting that that had provoked me to this *undue* severity. You . . . but I don't understand why, I can't help my confusion, and the colour that flushes my face at the thought of your suggestion – why, I can't speak directly and openly before her . . . In fact, you –'

'Oh, you wouldn't do that! No, don't say that!' cried Alexandra

Mikhailovna, burning with shame and greatly agitated. 'No, spare her. It was all my fault, it was my idea! I have no suspicions now. Forgive me for them, forgive me. I'm ill, you must forgive me, only do not speak of it to her, do not ... Annetta,' she said, coming up to me, 'Annetta, go out of the room, quick, quick! He was joking; it's all my fault; it's a thoughtless joke ...'

'In fact, you were jealous of her on my account,' said Pyotr Alexandrovitch, ruthlessly spitting out the words in the face of her agonized suspense.

She gave a shriek, turned pale and leaned against her chair for support, hardly able to stand on her feet.

'God forgive you,' she said at last in a faint voice. 'Forgive me for him, Netochka, forgive me; it was all my fault, I was ill, I –'

'But this is tyrannical, shameless, horrible!' I screamed, understanding it all at last. Now I could see why he wanted to discredit me before his wife. 'It's beneath contempt, you –'

'Annetta!' cried Alexandra Mikhailovna, seizing my hand in horror.

'It's a farce, a farce and nothing else!' said Pyotr Alexandrovitch, coming towards us in indescribable agitation. 'It's a farce, I tell you,' he went on, looking at his wife with a vindictive smile. 'And the only one who has been deceived by all this is you! I assure you that *we*,' he continued breathlessly, pointing at me, 'are not at all afraid of discussing such matters. Believe me, *we* are not so innocent as to be offended, to blush and cover our ears when someone starts talking to us of such matters. You must excuse me: I express myself plainly, simply, coarsely perhaps, but it is necessary. Are you so sure, madam, of the style of this ... young person's conduct?'

'My God! What's the matter with you? You're forgetting yourself!' said Alexandra Mikhailovna, numbed and half dead with horror.

'Not so loud, please,' Pyotr Alexandrovitch interrupted her contemptuously. 'I don't like it. This is a simple matter, plain and vulgar in the extreme. I'm asking you about her behaviour. Do you know –'

But I did not let him finish and, seizing him by the arm, I forcibly dragged him away. Another minute and all might have been lost.

'Don't mention the letter,' I whispered quickly. 'You will kill her on the spot. To reproach me is the same as reproaching her. She cannot be my judge because . . . I know everything . . . do you understand, *everything*!' He stared at me with wild curiosity. He was confused, the blood rushing to his face.

'I know *everything, everything*!' I repeated. He was still hesitant. A question was trembling on his lips, but I pre-empted him.

'This is what happened . . .' I began hurriedly to speak aloud, addressing Alexandra Mikhailovna, who was looking at us in timid, anxious amazement. 'It was all my fault. I have been deceiving you all, for the last four years. I took away the key of the library, and for four years I've been secretly reading the books inside. Pyotr Alexandrovitch caught me reading a book which . . . could not, should not have been in my hands. In his anxiety over me he has exaggerated the danger! . . . But I am not trying to justify myself,' I hastened to add, noticing the mocking smile on his lips. 'I'm entirely guilty. The temptation was too great and, having once done wrong, I was ashamed to confess what I'd done . . . That's all, almost all that has passed between us.'

'Oh, how clever!' whispered Pyotr Alexandrovitch, who was standing near me.

Alexandra Mikhailovna listened to me intently, but there was an unmistakable note of distrust written across her face. She kept looking from me to her husband. A silence followed. I could hardly breathe. She let her head fall on her breast and hid her face in her hands, evidently considering and weighing every word I had spoken. At last she lifted her head and looked straight at me.

'Netochka, my child, I know that you're not capable of telling a lie,' she said. 'Is that all, absolutely all that happened?'

'Yes, all,' I answered.

'Was that all?' she asked her husband.

'Yes,' he answered, with an effort, 'all!'

I let out a sigh.

'On your word, Netochka?'

'Yes,' I answered without faltering.

But I could not help glancing at Pyotr Alexandrovitch. He laughed when he heard my answer. My face was hot; my dismay did not escape poor Alexandra Mikhailovna. There was a look of overwhelming, agonizing misery in her face.

'That's enough,' she said mournfully. 'I believe you; I cannot but believe you.'

'I think such a confession is sufficient,' said Pyotr Alexandrovitch. 'You have heard it now! What would you have me think?'

Alexandra Mikhailovna gave no answer. The scene was becoming increasingly intolerable.

'Tomorrow I shall inspect all the books,' Pyotr Alexandrovitch resumed. 'I don't know what else there was there, but –'

'But what book was she reading?' asked Alexandra Mikhailovna.

'What book? Answer!' he said, addressing me. 'You can *explain things* better than I can,' he said with hidden irony. I was flustered and could not utter a word. Alexandra Mikhailovna blushed and lowered her eyes. There was a long pause. Pyotr Alexandrovitch paced the room in vexation.

'I don't know what has passed between you,' Alexandra Mikhailovna began at last, hesitantly articulating each word. 'But if that *was* all,' she went on, trying to put a special significance into her voice, and attempting in her embarrassment to avoid her husband's disconcerting stare, 'if that *was* all, then I don't know what cause we have for grief or despair. *I* am more guilty than anyone – I alone – and it troubles me very much. I've neglected her education, and I ought to answer for it all. She must forgive me, and I cannot and dare not blame her. But again, what is there for us to be so upset about? The danger has passed. Look at her,' she went on, speaking more and more feelingly and casting a searching look at her husband. 'Look at her . . . has her unfortunate action scarred her? Can it be that I don't know her, my child, my darling daughter? Don't I know that her heart is pure and noble, and that in that pretty little head –' she drew me towards her and fondled me – 'there is clear, candid intelligence and a conscience that is afraid of deceit . . . Enough of this, my dear! Let's forget it! Surely there's something else that's distressing us; perhaps a shadow of animosity came over us for a moment. But let's dispel it with love, with goodness; let's put aside our worries. Perhaps we've been keeping things hidden, and for this I am to blame the most. I was the first to conceal something, when I started having suspicions, though God knows of what. My sick mind is to blame . . . but, since we have been open to some extent, you must both forgive me because . . . because indeed there was no great sin in what I suspected . . .'

As she said this she glanced slyly, her cheeks flushed, at her husband and nervously awaited his response. While he listened to her a derisory smile came on to his lips. He ceased pacing the room and stood directly in front of her with his hands clasped behind his back; he was apparently contemplating her confusion, even delighting in it. Under his stare her anxiety deepened. He waited a moment as if he was expecting something more. Finally he cut short the uncomfortable scene with a soft, jeering laugh.

'You poor woman, I do feel sorry for you,' he said at last in a grave, bitter voice. He was no longer smiling. 'You have adopted an attitude which you can't keep up. What did you want? You wanted to incite me to answer, to rouse me with fresh suspicions, or rather with the old suspicion which you have failed to conceal with your words. The implication of what you say is that there is no need to be angry with her; that she's upright even after reading immoral books, which – I speak my feelings – seem already to have borne some fruit; that you're the one who is in fact responsible . . . Is that what you mean? Well, in explaining that, you hint at something else. You seem to think that my suspicions and my inquiries arise from another sort of feeling. You even implied yesterday – please do not interrupt, I wish to speak plainly – you even implied that in certain people (I remember that you said that such people are usually steady, severe, straightforward, intelligent, strong, and God knows what other attributes you gave them in your fit of magnanimity) ... that in certain people, I repeat, love – and God knows where you got this idea from – can only show itself vehemently, harshly and grimly, often in the form of suspicions and persecutions. I don't quite remember if that is exactly what you said yesterday ... please don't interrupt. I know your protégée well: she can hear all of this, *all of it* – I repeat for the hundredth time, all of it. You are decieved. But I don't know why you like to persuade yourself that I'm that sort of a person. God knows, you enjoy making a fool of me. I am hardly of an age to love that girl, and for that matter, you may rest assured, madam, that I *know my duty*, and however generously you may excuse me, I shall say as before, that *crime will always remain crime, that sin will always be sin: shameful, vile, dishonourable, to whatever height of grandeur you raise the vicious feeling*! But enough, enough, and let me hear no more of these abominations!'

Alexandra Mikhailovna was crying. 'Well, let *me* suffer this, let this be for *me*!' she said at last, sobbing and embracing me. 'My suspicions may have been shameful, you may well taunt me so ... but you, my poor child, why have you been condemned to listen to such insults? And I'm helpless to defend you! I'm speechless! My God!, I can't be silent! Sir, I can't endure this ... Your behaviour is insane.'

'Hush, hush,' I whispered, trying to soothe her agitation and afraid that her bitter reproaches would make him lose his patience. I was still quivering with fear for her.

'But, you blind woman!' he shouted. 'You know nothing, you see nothing!'

He paused for a moment.

'Away from her!' he said to me, and tore my hand from those of Alexandra Mikhailovna. 'I will not allow you to touch my wife; you pollute her, your presence is an insult to her. But ... but what is it that forces me to be silent when it is necessary – yes, essential – to speak?' he cried, stamping his foot. 'And I shall speak, I shall say everything. I have no idea what you *know*, madam, and with what you were trying to threaten me, nor do I wish to know. But listen to this,' he said, addressing his wife, 'just listen –'

'Be silent!' I cried, darting forwards. 'Hold your tongue, not a word!'

'Listen! . . .'

'Hold your tongue in the name of –'

'In the name of what, madam?' he interrupted, with a swift, penetrating look into my eyes. 'In the name of what? . . . Let me tell you, I took from her hands a letter from a lover! So that's what's going on in our house! That's what's happening at your side! That's what you've failed to notice, or even to see!'

I could barely stand up. Alexandra Mikhailovna had turned as white as a sheet.

'It cannot be,' she whispered in a voice hardly audible.

'I have seen this letter, madam; it's been in my hands. I read the first lines and there can be no mistake: the letter was from a lover. She snatched it away from me. She has it now, that's clear; it's true, there can be no doubt of it. If you still doubt it, just look at her and you'll see there is no question about it.'

'Netochka!' cried Alexandra Mikhailovna, rushing over to me. 'Ah, no, no, don't speak! I don't know what . . . how it . . . Oh, my God! My God!' And she buried her face in her hands and sobbed.

'But no, it cannot be,' she cried again, 'you're mistaken! I know . . . I know what it means,' she said, looking straight at her husband. 'You . . . I . . . could not . . . you're not deceiving me. Tell me all, don't hide anything. He's made a mistake. Yes, he's made a mistake, hasn't he? He's seen something else, he was blind! He was, wasn't he? Yes, he was. Why did you not tell me about it before, Netochka, my child, my own child?'

'Answer, answer immediately!' I heard Pyotr Alexandrovitch's voice above my head. 'Answer! Did I or did I not see the letter in your hands?'

'Yes!' I answered, breathless with emotion.

'Is the letter from your lover?'

'Yes!' I answered.

'With whom you are carrying out an intrigue?'

'Yes, yes, yes!' I said, hardly knowing what I was doing by now, and answering yes to every question, simply to put an end to our agony.

169

.'You heard her. Well, what do you say now? Believe me, your soul is too kind and trusting,' he added, taking his wife's hand. 'Believe me, and don't be deluded by all that your sick imagination has created. Now you see what this ... young person is. I only wanted to show you how impossible your suspicions were. I noticed all this long ago, and I'm glad to have at last unmasked her before you. It was disagreeable to me to see her beside you, in your arms, sitting at the same table as us, in my house, indeed. I was outraged by your blindness and that's the reason, the only reason, that I kept a watch on her; my attention attracted your notice and, starting from God knows what suspicions, you've deduced something or other from it. But now the position is clear, all doubt is settled, and tomorrow, madam, tomorrow you will leave my house,' he concluded, turning to me.

'Stop!' screeched Alexandra Mikhailovna, half rising from her chair. 'I don't believe all this. Don't look at me so fiercely, and don't mock me! I want to judge *you* now. Annetta, my child, come to me; give me your hand. We are all sinners!' she said in a voice that shook with tears, and looking meekly at her husband. 'And which of us can refuse another's hand? Give me your hand, Annetta, my dear child. I am no worthier, no better than you. You can't harm me with your presence, for I too, *I too am a sinner.*'

'Madam!' cried Pyotr Alexandrovitch in amazement. 'Madam, restrain yourself! Do not forget –'

'I forget nothing. Don't interrupt me ... let me finish. You saw a letter in her hands; you even read it. You say, and she too admits it, that it was a letter from someone she loves. But does this really prove that she's a criminal? Does it justify your treating her like this, degrading her in the eyes of your wife? Yes, sir, in the eyes of your wife. Have you perhaps considered the matter? And do you really know how it happened?'

'So, the only thing is for me to run and beg her pardon. Is that what you want?' cried Pyotr Alexandrovitch. 'I no longer have the patience to listen to you! Think what you're saying. Do you know what you're saying? Do you know what and whom you are defending? Why, I can see through all of it –'

'You fail to see the first thing; your pride and your anger prevent it. You can see neither what I'm defending nor what I'm trying to say. I'm not defending vice. But have you considered – and you'll see clearly if you do consider – have you considered that perhaps she's as innocent as a child? No, I'm not defending vice! I shall explain myself at once, if it gives you satisfaction. Yes, if she had been a wife and a mother and had forgotten her duties – oh, then I would have agreed with you . . . You see, I make a reservation. Take note of that and don't reproach me. But supposing she's received this letter without knowing it's wrong? What if she's been carried away by her inexperience and has had no one to guide her? Perhaps I'm the most guilty because I didn't watch over her heart. Was this the first letter? Perhaps it was, and you have insulted her fragrant, maidenly feelings with your coarse suspicions. What if you have sullied her imagination with your cruel talk about the letter? Could you not see that chaste, maidenly shame glowing in her face, pure as the innocence which I can see now and which I saw before, when you mortified and tortured her so that, not knowing what to say and torn with anguish, she answered by admitting to your cruel, inhuman accusations? Yes, yes! Yes, it's inhuman; it's cruel. I don't know you any more. I shall never forgive you for this, never!'

'Have mercy on me, have mercy!' I cried, clinging to her. 'Have mercy, trust me, don't reject me! . . .' I fell on my knees at her feet.

'What if, in fact,' she continued in a choked voice, 'I had not been at her side, and you had terrified her with your words and made the poor child believe she was guilty – confusing her conscience and soul, and shattering the peace of her heart? My God! You mean to turn her out of the house? Do you know who is treated like that? You know that if you turn her out of the house, you turn us out together, the two of us! Do you hear me, sir?' Her eyes flashed, her breast heaved; her feverish excitement reached a climax.

'Yes, I've heard enough, madam!' Pyotr Alexandrovitch finally shouted. 'Enough of this! I know that there are such things as platonic passions, and it's to my sorrow that I know it, madam, do you hear? To my sorrow. But I can't put up with gilded sin. I don't understand it. Put an end to trumpery! And if you feel that you are guilty, if you are aware of some wrong-doing on your part (it's not for me to remind you of it, madam) – if, in fact, you like the idea of leaving my house ... there's nothing left for me to say, but that you made a mistake in neglecting to carry out your intention at the proper time. If you have forgotten how many years ago it was; I will help you ...'

I glanced at Alexandra Mikhailovna. She was leaning over me and clutching at me convulsively, helpless with an inner agony, half closing her eyes in intense misery. Another minute and she would have collapsed.

'Oh, for God's sake, if only this once, spare her! Don't utter the final words!' I cried, falling at Pyotr Alexandrovitch's feet, and forgetting that I was betraying myself. But it was too late. A faint scream greeted my words, and the poor woman fell senseless to the floor.

'It's all over! You've killed her,' I said. 'Call the servants, save her! I'll wait for you in your study. I must speak to you; I'll tell you everything ...'

'But what? But what?'

'Later.'

The fainting and hysterics lasted two hours. The whole household was alarmed. The doctor shook his head doubtfully. After another two hours I went to Pyotr Alexandrovitch's study. He had only just come back from seeing his wife and was pacing the room, pale and distracted, biting his nails until they bled. I had never seen him in such a state.

'What do you want to say to me?' he said in a harsh, abrupt voice. 'Do you want to say something?'

'Here is the letter you snatched from my hands. Do you recognize it?'

'Yes.'

'Take it.'

He took the letter and raised it to the light. I watched him carefully. A few minutes later he reached the signature on the last page. I saw the blood rushing to his head.

'Well, what is it?' he asked, petrified with amazement.

'Three years ago I found this letter in a book. I presumed it had been forgotten; I read it and learnt everything. Since then it has been in my possession because I had no one to whom I could give it. I could not give it to her. Could I have given it to you? But you must have known the contents of this letter, the whole sorrowful story inside . . . I don't know why you're pretending. It's a mystery to me. I still can't understand your dark soul. You wanted to keep up your superiority over her and you have done so. But for what purpose? In order to triumph over a ghost, over the distraught imagination of a sick woman? To prove to her that she has erred and that you are more sinless than she? And you've achieved your aim, for this is the fixed idea of a failing mind, perhaps the last lament of a broken heart over the injustice of people's condemnation, with which you were in agreement. "What does it matter if you have fallen in love with her?" That is what she was saying and what she wanted to show you. Your vanity and your jealous egocentricity have been merciless. Farewell! There's no need to explain! But mind, I know you, I can see through you, don't forget that!'

I went to my room, hardly knowing what was happening to me. At the door I was stopped by Ovrov, Pyotr Alexandrovitch's secretary.

'I should like to have a word with you,' he said with a polite bow.

I looked at him, scarcely understanding what he had said to me.

'Later – excuse me, I'm not well,' I answered at last, walking past him.

'All right, tomorrow,' he said with a knowing smile. But perhaps I only imagined it. All this seemed to flit before my eyes.

FOR THE BEST IN PAPERBACKS, LOOK FOR THE

In every corner of the world, on every subject under the sun, Penguin represents quality and variety – the very best in publishing today.

For complete information about books available from Penguin – including Puffins, Penguin Classics and Arkana – and how to order them, write to us at the appropriate address below. Please note that for copyright reasons the selection of books varies from country to country.

In the United Kingdom: Please write to *Dept E.P., Penguin Books Ltd, Harmondsworth, Middlesex, UB7 0DA.*

If you have any difficulty in obtaining a title, please send your order with the correct money, plus ten per cent for postage and packaging, to *PO Box No 11, West Drayton, Middlesex*

In the United States: Please write to *Dept BA, Penguin, 299 Murray Hill Parkway, East Rutherford, New Jersey 07073*

In Canada: Please write to *Penguin Books Canada Ltd, 2801 John Street, Markham, Ontario L3R 1B4*

In Australia: Please write to the *Marketing Department, Penguin Books Australia Ltd, P.O. Box 257, Ringwood, Victoria 3134*

In New Zealand: Please write to the *Marketing Department, Penguin Books (NZ) Ltd, Private Bag, Takapuna, Auckland 9*

In India: Please write to *Penguin Overseas Ltd, 706 Eros Apartments, 56 Nehru Place, New Delhi, 110019*

In the Netherlands: Please write to *Penguin Books Netherlands B.V., Postbus 195, NL–1380AD Weesp*

In West Germany: Please write to *Penguin Books Ltd, Friedrichstrasse 10–12, D–6000 Frankfurt/Main 1*

In Spain: Please write to *Alhambra Longman S.A., Fernandez de la Hoz 9, E–28010 Madrid*

In Italy: Please write to *Penguin Italia s.r.l., Via Como 4, I-20096 Pioltello (Milano)*

In France: Please write to *Penguin Books Ltd, 39 Rue de Montmorency, F-75003 Paris*

In Japan: Please write to *Longman Penguin Japan Co Ltd, Yamaguchi Building, 2–12–9 Kanda Jimbocho, Chiyoda-Ku, Tokyo 101*

Anton Chekhov	The Duel and Other Stories
	The Kiss and Other Stories
	Lady with Lapdog and Other Stories
	Plays (The Cherry Orchard/Ivanov/The Seagull/Uncle Vanya/The Bear/The Proposal/A Jubilee/Three Sisters
	The Party and Other Stories
Fyodor Dostoyevsky	The Brothers Karamazov
	Crime and Punishment
	The Devils
	The Gambler/Bobok/A Nasty Story
	The House of the Dead
	The Idiot
	Netochka Nezvanova
	Notes From Underground and The Double
Nikolai Gogol	Dead Souls
	Diary of a Madman and Other Stories
Maxim Gorky	My Apprenticeship
	My Childhood
	My Universities
Mikhail Lermontov	A Hero of Our Time
Alexander Pushkin	Eugene Onegin
	The Queen of Spades and Other Stories
Leo Tolstoy	Anna Karenin
	Childhood/Boyhood/Youth
	The Cossacks/The Death of Ivan Ilyich/Happy Ever After
	The Kreutzer Sonata and Other Stories
	Master and Man and Other Stories
	Resurrection
	The Sebastopol Sketches
	War and Peace
Ivan Turgenev	Fathers and Sons
	First Love